FROM SAND HILL TO PINE

SPECIAL LARGE PRINT EDITION
with easy-to-read text

BRET HARTE

Serenity
Publishers, LLC
ROCKVILLE, MARYLAND
2012

ISBN: 978-1-60450-971-7

NOTE

Serenity Publishers can custom create classic texts in large print

We can create new titles with text/margins to your specifications

Add your notes and create the book as you want it

Combine different classic texts in one volume

Produce an edition with a special introduction or an afterword

Add your footnotes

Visit **www.SerenityPublishers.com** &
www.ArcManor.com

or email **chandi@serenitypublishers.com**

Published by Serenity Publishers
An Arc Manor Company
P. O. Box 10339
Rockville, MD 20849-0339
www.SerenityPublishers.com

Printed in the United States of America/United Kingdom

Contents

A Niece of Snapshot Harry's

I

There was a slight jarring though the whole frame of the coach, a grinding and hissing from the brakes, and then a sudden jolt as the vehicle ran upon and recoiled from the taut pole-straps of the now arrested horses. The murmur of a voice in the road was heard, followed by the impatient accents of Yuba Bill, the driver.

"Wha-a-t? Speak up, can't ye?"

Here the voice uttered something in a louder key, but equally unintelligible to the now interested and fully awakened passengers.

One of them dropped the window nearest him and looked out. He could see the faint glistening of a rain-washed lantern near the wheelers' heads, mingling with the stronger coach lights, and the glow of a distant open cabin door through the leaves and branches of the roadside. The sound of falling rain on the roof, a soft swaying of wind-tossed trees, and an impatient movement on the box-seat were all they heard. Then Yuba Bill's voice rose again, apparently in answer to the other.

"Why, that's half a mile away!"

"Yes, but ye might have dropped onto it in the dark, and it's all on the down grade," responded the strange voice more audibly.

The passengers were now thoroughly aroused.

"What's up, Ned?" asked the one at the window of the nearest of two figures that had descended from the box.

"Tree fallen across the road," said Ned, the express-man, briefly.

"I don't see no tree," responded the passenger, leaning out of the window towards the obscurity ahead.

"Now, that's onfortnit!" said Yuba Bill grimly; "but ef any gentleman will only lend him an opery glass, mebbe he can see round the curve and over the other side o' the hill where it is. Now, then," addressing the stranger with the lantern, "bring along your axes, can't ye?"

"Here's one, Bill," said an officious outside passenger, producing the instrument he had taken from its strap in the boot. It was the "regulation" axe, beautifully shaped, highly polished, and utterly ineffective, as Bill well knew.

"We ain't cuttin' no kindlin's," he said scornfully; then he added brusquely to the stranger: "Fetch out your biggest wood axe—you've got one, ye know—and look sharp."

"I don't think Bill need be so d—d rough with the stranger, considering he's saved the coach a very bad smash," suggested a reflective young journalist in the next seat. "He talks as if the man was responsible."

6

"He ain't quite sure if that isn't the fact," said the express messenger, in a lowered voice.

"Why? What do you mean?" clamored the others excitedly.

"Well—*this* is about the spot where the up coach was robbed six months ago," returned the messenger.

"Dear me!" said the lady in the back seat, rising with a half hysterical laugh, "hadn't we better get out before they come?"

"There is not the slightest danger, madam," said a quiet, observant man, who had scarcely spoken before, "or the expressman would not have told us; nor would he, I fancy, have left his post beside the treasure on the box."

The slight sarcasm implied in this was enough to redden the expressman's cheek in the light of the coach lamp which Yuba Bill had just unshipped and brought to the window. He would have made some tart rejoinder, but was prevented by Yuba Bill addressing the passengers: "Ye'll have to put up with *one* light, I reckon, until we've got this job finished."

"How long will it last, Bill?" asked the man nearest the window.

"Well," said Bill, with a contemptuous glance at the elegant coach axe he was carrying in his hand, "considerin' these purty first-class highly expensive hash choppers that the kempany furnishes us, I reckon it may take an hour."

"But is there no place where we can wait?" asked the lady anxiously. "I see a light in that house yonder."

"Ye might try it, though the kempany, as a rule, ain't in the habit o' makin' social calls there," returned Bill, with a certain grim significance. Then, turning to some outside passengers, he added, "Now, then! them ez is goin' to help me tackle that tree, trot down! I reckon that blitherin' idiot" (the stranger with the lantern, who had disappeared) "will have sense enough to fetch us some ropes with his darned axe."

The passengers thus addressed, apparently miners and workingmen, good humoredly descended, all except one, who seemed disinclined to leave the much coveted seat on the box beside the driver.

"I'll look after your places and keep my own," he said, with a laugh, as the others followed Bill through the dripping rain. When they had disappeared, the young journalist turned to the lady.

"If you would really like to go to that house, I will gladly accompany you." It was possible that in addition to his youthful chivalry there was a little youthful resentment of Yuba Bill's domineering prejudices in his attitude. However, the quiet, observant passenger lifted a look of approval to him, and added, in his previous level, half contemptuous tone:—

"You'll be quite as well there as here, madam, and there is certainly no reason for your stopping in the coach when the driver chooses to leave it."

The passengers looked at each other. The stranger spoke with authority, and Bill had certainly been a little arbitrary!

"I'll go too," said the passenger by the window. "And you'll come, won't you, Ned?" he added to the express messenger. The young man hesitated; he was recently appointed, and as yet fresh to the business—but he was not to be taught his duty by an officious stranger! He resented the interference youthfully by doing the very thing he would have preferred *not* to do, and with assumed carelessness—yet feeling in his pocket to assure himself that the key of the treasure compartment was safe—turned to follow them.

"Won't *you* come too?" said the journalist, politely addressing the cynical passenger.

"No, I thank you! I'll take charge of the coach," was the smiling rejoinder, as he settled himself more comfortably in his seat.

The little procession moved away in silence. Oddly enough, no one, except the lady, really cared to go, and two—the expressman and journalist—would have preferred to remain on the coach. But the national instinct of questioning any purely arbitrary authority probably was a sufficient impulse. As they neared the opened door of what appeared to be a four-roomed, unpainted, redwood boarded cabin, the passenger who had occupied the seat near the window said,—

"I'll go first and sample the shanty."

He was not, however, so far in advance of them but that the others could hear quite distinctly his offhand introduction of their party on the threshold, and the somewhat lukewarm response of the inmates. "We thought we'd just drop in and be sociable until the coach was ready to start again," he continued, as the other passengers entered. "This yer gentleman is Ned Brice, Adams & Co.'s expressman; this yer is Frank Frenshaw, editor of the 'Mountain Banner;' this yer's a lady, so it ain't necessary to give *her* name, I reckon—even if we knowed it! Mine's Sam Hexshill, of Hexshill & Dobbs's Flour Mills, of Stockton, whar, ef you ever come that way, I'll be happy to return the compliment and hospitality."

The room they had entered had little of comfort and brightness in it except the fire of pine logs which roared and crackled in the adobe chimney. The air would have been too warm but for the strong west wind and rain which entered the open door freely. There was no other light than the fire, and its tremulous and ever-changing brilliancy gave a spasmodic mobility to the faces of those turned towards it, or threw into stronger shadow the features that were turned away. Yet, by this uncertain light, they could see the figures of a man and two women. The man rose and, with a certain apathetic gesture that seemed to partake more of weariness and long suffering than positive discourtesy, tendered seats on chairs, boxes, and even logs to the self-invited guests. The stage party were surprised to see that this man was the stranger who had held the lantern in the road.

"Ah! then you didn't go with Bill to help clear the road?" said the expressman surprisedly.

The man slowly drew up his tall, shambling figure before the fire, and then facing them, with his hands behind him, as slowly lowered himself again as if to bring his speech to the level of his hearers and give a lazier and more deliberate effect to his long-drawn utterance.

"Well—no!" he said slowly. "I—didn't—go—with—no—Bill—to—help—clear—the road! I—don't—reckon—*to* go—with—no—Bill—to—clear—*any* road! I've just whittled this thing down to a pint, and it's this—I ain't no stage kempany's nigger! So far as turnin' out and warnin' 'em agin goin' to smash over a fallen tree, and slap down into the canyon with a passel of innercent passengers, I'm that much a white man, but I ain't no *nigger* to work clearing things away for 'em, nor I ain't no scrub to work beside 'em." He slowly straightened himself up again, and, with his former apathetic air, looking down upon one of the women who was setting a coffee-pot on the coals, added, "But I reckon my old woman here kin give you some coffee and whiskey—of you keer for it."

Unfortunately the young expressman was more loyal to Bill than diplomatic. "If Bill's a little rough," he said, with a heightened color, "perhaps he has some excuse for it. You forget it's only six months ago that this coach was 'held up' not a hundred yards from this spot."

The woman with the coffee-pot here faced about, stood up, and, either from design or some odd coincidence, fell into the same dogged attitude that her husband had previously taken, except that she rested her hands on her hips. She was prematurely aged, like many of her class, and her black, snake-like locks, twisting loose from her comb as she lifted her head, showed threads of white against the firelight. Then with slow and implacable deliberation she said:

"We 'forget'! Well! not much, sonny! We ain't forgot it, and we ain't goin' to forget it, neither! We ain't bin likely to forget it for any time the last six months. What with visitations from the county constables, snoopin's round from 'Frisco detectives, droppin's-in from newspaper men, and yawpin's and starin's from tramps and strangers on the road—we haven't had a chance to disremember *much*! And when at last Hiram tackled the head stage agent at Marysville, and allowed that this yer pesterin' and persecutin' had got ter stop—what did that yer head agent tell him? Told him to 'shet his head,' and be thankful that his 'thievin' old shanty wasn't burnt down around his ears!' Forget that six months ago the coach was held up near here? Not much, sonny—not much!"

The situation was embarrassing to the guests, as ordinary politeness called for some expression of sympathy with their gloomy hostess, and yet a selfish instinct of humanity warned them that there must be some foundation for this general distrust of the public. The journalist was troubled in his conscience; the expressman took refuge in an official reticence; the lady coughed slightly, and drew nearer to the fire with a vague but safe compliment to its brightness and comfort. It devolved upon Mr. Heckshill, who felt the responsibility of his late airy introduction of the party, to boldly keep up his role, with an equally non-committal, light-hearted philosophy.

"Well, ma'am," he said, addressing his hostess, "it's a queer world, and no man's got sabe enough to say what's the rights and wrongs o' anything. Some folks believe one thing and act upon it, and other folks think differently and act upon *that*! The only thing ye kin safely say is that *things is ez they be*! My rule here and at the mill is jest to take things ez I find 'em!"

It occurred to the journalist that Mr. Heckshill had the reputation, in his earlier career, of "taking" such things as unoccupied lands and timber "as he found them," without much reference to their actual own-ers. Apparently he was acting upon the same principle now, as he reached for the demijohn of whiskey with the ingenuous pleasantry, "Did somebody say whiskey, or did I dream it?"

But this did not satisfy Frenshaw. "I suppose," he said, ignoring Heckshill's diplomatic philosophy, "that you may have been the victim of some misun-derstanding or some unfortunate coincidence. Per-haps the company may have confounded you with your neighbors, who are believed to be friendly to the gang; or you may have made some injudicious acquaintances. Perhaps"—

He was stopped by a suppressed but not unmusical giggle, which appeared to come from the woman in the corner who had not yet spoken, and whose face and figure in the shadow he had previously overlooked.

But he could now see that her outline was slim and graceful, and the contour of her head charming,— facts that had evidently not escaped the observation of the expressman and Mr. Heckshill, and that might have accounted for the cautious reticence of the one and the comfortable moralizing of the other.

The old woman cast an uneasy glance on the fair giggler, but replied to Frenshaw:

"That's it! 'injerdishus acquaintances!' But just because we might happen to have friends, or even be sorter related to folks in another line o' business that ain't none o' ours, the kempany hain't no call to persecute *us* for it! S'pose we do happen to know some one like"—

"Spit it out, aunty, now you've started in! I don't mind," said the fair giggler, now apparently casting off all restraint in an outburst of laughter.

"Well," said the old woman, with dogged desperation, "suppose, then, that that young girl thar is the niece of Snapshot Harry, who stopped the coach the last time"—

"And ain't ashamed of it, either!" interrupted the young girl, rising and disclosing in the firelight an audacious but wonderfully pretty face; "and supposing he IS my uncle, that ain't any cause for their bedevilin' my poor old cousins Hiram and Sophy thar!" For all the indignation of her words, her little white teeth flashed mischievously in the dancing light, as if she rather enjoyed the embarrassment of her audience, not excluding her own relatives. Evidently cousin Sophy thought so too.

"It's all very well for you to laugh, Flo, you limb!" she retorted querulously, yet with an admiring glance at the girl, "for ye know thar ain't a man dare touch ye even with a word; but it's mighty hard on me and Hiram, all the same."

"Never you mind, Sophy dear," said the girl, placing her hand half affectionately, half humorously on the old woman's shoulder; "mebbe I won't always be a discredit and a bother to you. Jest you hold your hosses, and wait until uncle Harry 'holds up' the next Pioneer Coach,"—the dancing devil in her eyes glanced as if accidentally on the young expressman,—"and he'll make a big enough pile to send me to Europe, and you'll be quit o' me."

The embarrassment, suspiciousness, and uneasiness of the coach party here found relief in a half hysteric explosion of laughter, in which even the dogged Hiram and Sophy joined. It seemed as impossible to withstand the girl's invincible audacity as her beauty. She was quick to perceive her advantage, and, with a responsive laugh and a picturesque gesture of invitation, said:—

"Now that's all settled, ye'd better waltz in and have your whiskey and coffee afore the stage starts. Ye kin comfort yourselves that it ain't stolen or pizoned, even if it is served up to ye by Snapshot Harry's niece!" With another easy gesture she swung the demijohn over her arm, and, offering a tin cup to each of the men, filled them in turn.

The ice thus broken, or perhaps thus perilously skated over, the passengers were as profuse in their thanks and apologies as they had been constrained and artificial before. Heckshill and Frenshaw vied with each other for a glance from the audacious Flo. If their compliments partook of an extravagance that was at times ironical, the girl was evidently not deceived by it, but replied in kind. Only the expressman who seemed to have fallen under the spell of her audacious glances, was uneasy at the license of the others, yet himself dumb towards her. The lady discreetly drew nearer to the fire, the old woman, and her coffee; Hiram subsided into his apathetic attitude by the fire.

A shout from the road at last proclaimed the return of Yuba Bill and his helpers. It had the singular effect of startling the party into a vague and uneasy consciousness of indiscretion, as if it had been the voice of the outer world of law and order, and their manner again became constrained. The leave-taking was hurried and perfunctory; the diplomatic Heckshill again lapsed into glittering generalities about "the best of friends parting." Only the expressman lingered for a moment on the doorstep in the light of the fire and the girl's dancing eyes.

"I hope," he stammered, with a very youthful blush, "to come the next time—with—with—a better introduction."

"Uncle Harry's," she said, with a quick laugh and a mock curtsey, as she turned away.

Once out of hearing, the party broke into hurried comment and criticism of the scene they had just witnessed, and particularly of the fair actress who had played so important a part, averring their emphatic intention of wresting the facts from Yuba Bill at once, and cross-examining him closely; but oddly enough, reaching the coach and that redoubted individual, no one seemed to care to take the initiative, and they all scrambled hurriedly to their seats without a word. How far Yuba Bill's irritability and imperious haste contributed to this, or a fear that he might in turn catechise them kept them silent, no one knew. The cynically observant passenger was not there; he and the sole occupant of the box-seat, they were told, had joined the clearing party some moments before, and would be picked up by Yuba Bill later on.

Five minutes after Bill had gathered up the reins, they reached the scene of obstruction. The great pine-tree which had fallen from the steep bank above and stretched across the road had been partly lopped of its branches, divided in two lengths, which were now rolled to either side of the track, leaving barely space for the coach to pass. The huge vehicle "slowed up" as Yuba Bill skillfully guided his six horses through this narrow alley, whose tassels of pine, glistening with wet, brushed the panels and sides of the coach, and effectually excluded any view from its windows. Seen from the coach top, the horses appeared to be cleaving their way through a dark, shining olive sea, that parted before and closed behind them, as they slowly passed. The leaders were just emerging from it, and Bill was gathering up his slackened reins, when a peremptory voice called, "Halt!" At the same moment the coach lights flashed upon a masked and motionless horseman in the road. Bill made an impulsive reach for his whip, but in the same instant checked himself, reined in his horses with a suppressed oath, and sat perfectly rigid. Not so the expressman, who caught up his rifle, but it was arrested by Bill's arm, and his voice in his ear!

"Too late!—we're covered!—don't be a d—d fool!"

The inside passengers, still encompassed by obscurity, knew only that the stage had stopped. The "outsiders" knew, by experience, that they were covered by unseen guns in the wayside branches, and scarcely moved.

"I didn't think it was the square thing to stop you, Bill, till you'd got through your work," said a masterful but not unpleasant voice, "and if you'll just hand down the express box, I'll pass you and the rest of your load through free. But as we're both in a hurry, you'd better look lively about it."

"Hand it down," said Bill gruffly to the expressman.

The expressman turned with a white check but blazing eyes to the compartment below his seat. He lingered, apparently in some difficulty with the lock of the compartment, but finally brought out the box and handed it to another armed and masked figure that appeared mysteriously from the branches beside the wheels.

"Thank you!" said the voice; "you can slide on now."

"And thank you for nothing," said Bill, gathering up his reins. "It's the first time any of your kind had to throw down a tree to hold me up!"

"You're lying, Bill!—though you don't know it," said the voice cheerfully. "Far from throwing down a tree to stop you, it was I sent word along the road to warn you from crashing down upon it, and sending you and your load to h-ll before your time! Drive on!"

The angry Bill waited for no second comment, but laying his whip over the backs of his team, drove furiously forward. So rapidly had the whole scene passed that the inside passengers knew nothing of it, and even those on the top of the coach roused from their stupor and inglorious inaction only to cling desperately to the terribly swaying coach as it thundered down the grade and try to keep their equilibrium. Yet, furious as was their speed, Yuba Bill could not help noticing that the expressman from time to time cast a hurried glance behind him. Bill knew that the young man had shown readiness and nerve in the attack, although both were hopeless; yet he was so much concerned at his set white face and compressed lips that when, at the end of three miles' unabated speed, they galloped up to the first station, he seized the young man by the arm, and, as the clamor of the news they had brought rose around them, dragged him past the wondering crowd, caught a decanter from the bar, and, opening the door of a side room, pushed him into it and closed the door behind them.

"Look yar, Brice! Stop it! Quit it right thar!" he said emphatically, laying his large hand on the young fellow's shoulder. "Be a man! You've shown you are one, green ez you are, for you had the sand in ye—the clear grit to-night, yet you'd have been a dead man now, if I hadn't stopped ye! Man! you had no show from the beginning! You've done your level best to save your treasure, and I'm your witness to the kempany, and proud of it, too! So shet your head and—and," pouring out a glass of whiskey, "swaller that!"

But Brice waved him aside with burning eyes and dry lips.

"You don't know it all, Bill!" he said, with a half choked voice.

"All what?"

"Swear that you'll keep it a secret," he said feverishly, gripping Bill's arm in turn, "and I'll tell you."

"Go on!"

"The coach was robbed before that!"

"Wot yer say?" ejaculated Bill.

"The treasure—a packet of greenbacks—had been taken from the box before the gang stopped us!"

"The h-ll, you say!"

"Listen! When you told me to hand down the box, I had an idea—a d—d fool one, perhaps—of taking that package out and jumping from the coach with it. I knew they would fire at me only; I might get away, but if they killed me, I'd have done only my duty, and nobody else would have got hurt. But when I got to the box I found that the lock had been forced and the money was gone. I managed to snap the lock again before I handed it down. I thought they might discover it at once and chase us, but they didn't."

"And then thar war no greenbacks in the box that they took?" gasped Bill, with staring eyes.

"No!"

Bill raised his hand in the air as if in solemn adjuration, and then brought it down on his knee, doubling up in a fit of uncontrollable but perfectly noiseless laughter. "Oh, Lord!" he gasped, "hol' me afore I bust right open! Hush," he went on, with a jerk of his fingers towards the next room, "not a word o' this to any one! It's too much to keep, I know; it's nearly killing me! but we must swaller it ourselves! Oh, Jerusalem the Golden! Oh, Brice! Think o' that face o' Snapshot Harry's ez he opened that treasure box afore his gang in the brush! And he allers so keen and so easy and so cock sure! Created snakes! I'd go through this every trip for one sight of him as he just riz up from that box and cussed!" He again shook with inward convulsions till his face grew purple, and even the red came back to the younger man's cheek.

"But this don't bring the money back, Bill," said Brice gloomily.

Yuba Bill swallowed the glass of whiskey at a gulp, wiped his mouth and eyes, smothered a second explosion, and then gravely confronted Brice.

"When do you think it was taken, and how?"

"It must have been taken when I left the coach on the road and went over to that settler's cabin," said Brice bitterly. "Yet I believed everything was safe, and I left two men—both passengers—one inside and one on the box, that man who sat the other side of you."

"Jee whillikins!" ejaculated Bill, with his hand to his forehead, "the men I clean forgot to pick up in the road, and now I reckon they never intended to be picked up, either."

"No doubt a part of the gang," said Brice, with increased bitterness; "I see it all now."

"No!" said Bill decisively, "that ain't Snapshot Harry's style; he's a clean fighter, with no underhand tricks. And I don't believe he threw down that tree, either. Look yer, sonny!" he added, suddenly laying his hand on Brice's shoulder, "a hundred to one that that was the work of a couple o' d—d sneaks or traitors in that gang who kem along as passengers. I never took any stock in that coyote who paid extra for his box-seat."

Brice knew that Bill never looked kindly on any passenger who, by bribing the ticket agent, secured this favorite seat, which Bill felt was due to his personal friends and was in his own selection. He only returned gloomily:—

"I don't see what difference it makes to us which robber got the money.

"Ye don't," said Bill, raising his head, with a sudden twinkle in his eyes. "Then ye don't know Snapshot Harry. Do ye suppose he's goin' to sit down and twiddle his thumbs with that skin game played on him? No, sir," he continued, with a thoughtful deliberation, drawing his fingers slowly through his long beard, "he spotted it—and smelt out the whole trick ez soon ez he opened that box, and that's why he didn't foller us! He'll hunt those sneak thieves into h-ll but what he'll get 'em, and," he went on still more slowly, "by the livin' hokey! I reckon, sonny, that's jest how ye'll get your chance to chip in!"

"I don't understand," said Brice impatiently.

"Well," said Bill, with more provoking slowness, as if he were communing with himself rather than Brice, "Harry's mighty proud and high toned, and to be given away like this has cut down into his heart, you bet. It ain't the money he's thinkin' of; it's this split in the gang—the loss of his power ez boss, ye see—and ef he could get hold o' them chaps he'd let the money slide ez long ez they didn't get it. So you've got a detective on your side that's worth the whole police force of Californy! Ye never heard anything about Snapshot Harry, did ye?" asked Bill carelessly, raising his eyes to Brice's eager face.

The young man flushed slightly. "Very little," he said. At the same time a vision of the pretty girl in the settler's cabin flashed upon him with a new significance.

"He's more than half white, in some ways," said Bill thoughtfully, "and they say he lives somewhere about here in a cabin in the bush, with a crippled sister and her darter, who both swear by him. It mightn't be hard to find him—ef a man was dead set on it."

Brice faced about with determined eyes. "*I'll do it*," he said quietly.

"Ye might," said Bill, still more deliberately stroking his beard, "mention my name, ef ye ever get to see him."

"Your name," ejaculated the astonished Brice.

"My name," repeated Bill calmly. "He knows it's my bounden duty to kill him ef I get the chance, and I know that he'd plug me full o' holes in a minit ef thar war a necessity for it. But in these yer affairs, sonny, it seems to be the understood thing by the kempany that I'm to keep fiery young squirts like you, and chuckle-headed passengers like them"—jerking his thumb towards the other room—"from gettin' themselves killed by their rashness. So ontil the kempany fill the top o' that coach with men who ain't got any business to do *but* fightin' other men who ain't got any other business to do *but* to fight them—the odds are agin us! Harry has always acted square to me—that's how I know he ain't in this sneak-thief business, and why he didn't foller us, suspectin' suthin', and I've always acted square to him. All the same, I'd like ter hev seen his face when that box was opened! Lordy!" Here Bill again collapsed in his silent paroxysm of mirth. "Ye might tell him how I laughed!"

"I would hardly do that, Bill," said the young man, smiling in spite of himself. "But you've given me an idea, and I'll work it out."

Bill glanced at the young fellow's kindling eyes and flushing cheek, and nodded. "Well, rastle with that idea later on, sonny. I'll fix you all right in my report to the kempany, but the rest you must work alone. I've started out the usual posse, circus-ridin' down the road after Harry. He'd be a rough customer to meet just now," continued Bill, with a chuckle, "ef thar was the ghost of a chance o' them comin' up with him, for him and his gang is scattered miles away by this." He paused, tossed off another glass of whiskey, wiped his mouth, and saying to Brice, with a wink, "It's about time to go and comfort them thar passengers," led the way through the crowded barroom into the stage office.

The spectacle of Bill's humorously satisfied face and Brice's bright eyes and heightened color was singularly effective. The "inside" passengers, who had experienced neither the excitement nor the danger of the robbery, yet had been obliged to listen to the hairbreadth escapes of the others, pooh-poohed the whole affair, and even the "outsides" themselves were at last convinced that the robbery was a slight one, with little or no loss to the company. The clamor subsided almost as suddenly as it had arisen; the wiser passengers fashioned their attitude on the sang-froid of Yuba Bill, and the whole coach load presently rolled away as complacently as if nothing had happened.

II

The robbery furnished the usual amount of copy for the local press. There was the inevitable compliment to Yuba Bill for his well-known coolness; the conduct of the young expressman, "who, though new to the service, displayed an intrepidity that only succumbed to numbers," was highly commended, and even the passengers received their meed of praise, not forgetting the lady, "who accepted the incident with the light-hearted pleasantry characteristic of the Californian woman." There was the usual allusion to the necessity of a Vigilance Committee to cope with this "organized lawlessness" but it is to be feared that the readers of "The Red Dog Clarion," however ready to lynch a horse thief, were of the opinion that rich stage express companies were quite able to take care of their own property.

It was with full cognizance of these facts and their uselessness to him that the next morning Mr. Ned Brice turned from the road where the coach had just halted on the previous night and approached the settler's cabin. If a little less sanguine than he was in Yuba Bill's presence, he was still doggedly inflexible in his design, whatever it might have been, for he had not revealed it even to Yuba Bill. It was his own; it was probably crude and youthful in its directness, but for that reason it was probably more convincing than the vacillations of older counsel.

He paused a moment at the closed door, conscious, however, of some hurried movement within which signified that his approach had been observed. The door was opened, and disclosed only the old woman. The same dogged expression was on her face as when he had last seen it, with the addition of querulous expectancy. In reply to his polite "Good-morning," she abruptly faced him with her hands still on the door.

"Ye kin stop right there! Ef yer want ter make any talk about this yar robbery, ye might ez well skedaddle to oncet, for we ain't 'takin' any' to-day!"

"I have no wish to talk about the robbery," said Brice quietly, "and as far as I can prevent it, you will not be troubled by any questions. If you doubt my word or the intentions of the company, perhaps you will kindly read that."

He drew from his pocket a still damp copy of "The Red Dog Clarion" and pointed to a paragraph.

"Wot's that?" she said querulously, feeling for her spectacles.

"Shall I read it?"

"Go on."

He read it slowly aloud. I grieve to say it had been jointly concocted the night before at the office of the "Clarion" by himself and the young journalist—the latter's assistance being his own personal tribute to the graces of Miss Flo. It read as follows:—

"The greatest assistance was rendered by Hiram Tarbox, Esq., a resident of the vicinity, in removing the obstruction, which was, no doubt, the preliminary work of some of the robber gang, and in providing hospitality for the delayed passengers.

In fact, but for the timely warning of Yuba Bill by Mr. Tarbox, the coach might have crashed into the tree at that dangerous point, and an accident ensued more disastrous to life and limb than the robbery itself."

The sudden and unmistakable delight that expanded the old woman's mouth was so convincing that it might have given Brice a tinge of remorse over the success of his stratagem, had he not been utterly absorbed in his purpose. "Hiram!" she shouted suddenly.

The old man appeared from some back door with a promptness that proved his near proximity, and glanced angrily at Brice until he caught sight of his wife's face. Then his anger changed to wonder.

"Read that again, young feller," she said exultingly.

Brice re-read the paragraph aloud for Mr. Tarbox's benefit.

"That 'ar 'Hiram Tarbox, Esquire,' means *you*, Hiram," she gasped, in delighted explanation.

Hiram seized the paper, read the paragraph himself, spread out the whole page, examined it carefully, and then a fatuous grin began slowly to extend itself over his whole face, invading his eyes and ears, until the heavy, harsh, dogged lines of his nostrils and jaws had utterly disappeared.

"B'gosh!" he said, "that's square! Kin I keep it?"

"Certainly," said Brice. "I brought it for you."

"Is that all ye came for?" said Hiram, with sudden suspicion.

"No," said the young man frankly. Yet he hesitated a moment as he added, "I would like to see Miss Flora."

His hesitation and heightened color were more disarming to suspicion than the most elaborate and carefully prepared indifference. With their knowledge and pride in their relative's fascinations they felt it could have but one meaning! Hiram wiped his mouth with his hand, assumed a demure expression, glanced at his wife, and answered:—

"She ain't here now."

Mr. Brice's face displayed his disappointment. But the true lover holds a talisman potent with old and young. Mrs. Tarbox felt a sneaking maternal pity for this suddenly stricken Strephon.

"She's gone home," she added more gently—"went at sun-up this mornin'."

"Home," repeated Brice. "Where's that?"

Mrs. Tarbox looked at her husband and hesitated. Then she said—a little in her old manner—"Her uncle's."

"Can you direct me the way there?" asked Brice simply.

The astonishment in their faces presently darkened into suspicion again. "Ef that's your little game," began Hiram, with a lowering brow—

"I have no little game but to see her and speak with her," said Brice boldly. "I am alone and unarmed, as you see," he continued, pointing to his empty belt and small dispatch bag slung on his shoulder, "and certainly unable to do any one any harm. I am willing to take what risks there are. And as no one knows of my intention, nor of my coming here, whatever might happen to me, no one need know it. You would be safe from questioning."

There was that hopeful determination in his manner that overrode their resigned doggedness. "Ef we knew how to direct you thar," said the old woman cautiously, "ye'd be killed outer hand afore ye even set eyes on the girl. The house is in a holler with hills kept by spies; ye'd be a dead man as soon as ye crossed its boundary."

"Wot do *you* know about it?" interrupted her husband quickly, in querulous warning. "Wot are ye talkin' about?"

"You leave me alone, Hiram! I ain't goin' to let that young feller get popped off without a show, or without knowin' jest wot he's got to tackle, nohow ye kin fix it! And can't ye see he's bound to go, whatever ye says?"

Mr. Tarbox saw this fact plainly in Brice's eyes, and hesitated.

"The most that I kin tell ye," he said gloomily, "is the way the gal takes when she goes from here, but how far it is, or if it ain't a blind, I can't swar, for I hevn't bin thar myself, and Harry never comes here but on an off night, when the coach ain't runnin' and thar's no travel." He stopped suddenly and uneasily, as if he had said too much.

"Thar ye go, Hiram, and ye talk of others gabblin'! So ye might as well tell the young feller how that thar ain't but one way, and that's the way Harry takes, too, when he comes yer oncet in an age to talk to his own flesh and blood, and see a Christian face that ain't agin him!"

Mr. Tarbox was silent. "Ye know whar the tree was thrown down on the road," he said at last.

"Yes."

"The mountain rises straight up on the right side of the road, all hazel brush and thorn—whar a goat couldn't climb."

"Yes."

"But that's a lie! for thar's a little trail, not a foot wide, runs up from the road for a mile, keepin' it in view all the while, but bein' hidden by the brush. Ye kin see everything from thar, and hear a teamster spit on the road."

"Go on," said Brice impatiently.

"Then it goes up and over the ridge, and down the other side into a little gulch until it comes to the canyon of the North Fork, where the stage road crosses over the bridge high up. The trail winds round the bank of the Fork and comes out on the *left* side of the stage road about a thousand feet below it. That's the valley and hollow whar Harry lives, and that's the only way it can be found. For all along the *left* of the stage road is a sheer pitch down that thousand feet, whar no one kin git up or down."

"I understand," said Brice, with sparkling eyes. "I'll find my way all right."

"And when ye git thar, look out for yourself!" put in the woman earnestly. "Ye may have regular greenhorn's luck and pick up Flo afore ye cross the boundary, for she's that bold that when she gets lone-some o' stayin' thar she goes wanderin' out o' bounds."

"Hev ye any weppin,—any shootin'-iron about ye?" asked Tarbox, with a latent suspicion.

The young man smiled, and again showed his emp-ty belt. "None!" he said truthfully.

"I ain't sure ef that ain't the safest thing arter all with a shot like Harry," remarked the old man grimly. "Well, so long!" he added, and turned away.

It was clearly a leave-taking, and Brice, warmly thanking them both, returned to the road.

It was not far to the scene of the obstruction, yet but for Tarbox's timely hint, the little trail up the mountain side would have escaped his observation. Ascending, he soon found himself creeping along a narrow ledge of rock, hidden from the road that ran fifty yards below by a thick network growth of thorn and bramble, which still enabled him to see its whole parallel length. Perilous in the extreme to any hesitat-ing foot, at one point, directly above the obstruction, the ledge itself was missing—broken away by the fall of the tree from the forest crest higher up. For an in-stant Brice stood dizzy and irresolute before the gap. Looking down for a foothold, his eye caught the faint imprint of a woman's shoe on a clayey rock projecting midway of the chasm. It must have been the young girl's footprint made that morning, for the narrow toe was pointed in the direction she would go! Where *she* could pass should he shrink from going? Without further hesitation he twined his fingers around the roots above him, and half swung, half pulled himself along until he once more felt the ledge below him.

From time to time, as he went on along the difficult track, the narrow little toe-print pointed the way to him, like an arrow through the wilds. It was a pleasant thought, and yet a perplexing one. Would he have undertaken this quest just to see her? Would he be content with that if his other motive failed? For as he made his way up to the ridge he was more than once assailed by doubts of the practical success of his enterprise. In the excitement of last night, and even the hopefulness of the early morning, it seemed an easy thing to persuade the vain and eccentric highwayman that their interests might be identical, and to convince him that his, Brice's, assistance to recover the stolen greenbacks and insure the punishment of the robber, with the possible addition of a reward from the express company, would be an inducement for them to work together. The risks that he was running seemed to his youthful fancy to atone for any defects in his logic or his plans. Yet as he crossed the ridge, leaving the civilized highway behind him, and descended the narrow trail, which grew wilder at each step, his arguments seemed no longer so convincing. He now hurried forward, however, with a feverish haste to anticipate the worst that might befall him.

The trail grew more intricate in the deep ferns; the friendly little footprint had vanished in this primeval wilderness. As he pushed through the gorge, he could hear at last the roar of the North Fork forcing its way through the canyon that crossed the gorge at right angles. At last he reached its current, shut in by two narrow precipitous walls that were spanned five hundred feet above by the stage road over a perilous bridge. As he approached the gloomy canyon, he remembered that the river, seen from above, seemed to have no banks, but to have cut its way through the solid rock.

He found, however, a faint ledge made by caught driftwood from the current and the debris of the overhanging cliffs. Again the narrow footprint on the ooze was his guide. At last, emerging from the canyon, a strange view burst upon his sight. The river turned abruptly to the right, and, following the mountain side, left a small hollow completely walled in by the surrounding heights. To his left was the ridge he had descended from on the other side, and he now understood the singular detour he had made. He was on the other side of the stage road also, which ran along the mountain shelf a thousand feet above him. The wall, a sheer cliff, made the hollow inaccessible from that side. Little hills covered with buckeye encompassed it. It looked like a sylvan retreat, and yet was as secure in its isolation and approaches as the outlaw's den that it was.

He was gazing at the singular prospect when a shot rang in the air. It seemed to come from a distance, and he interpreted it as a signal. But it was followed presently by another; and putting his hand to his hat to keep it from falling, he found that the upturned brim had been pierced by a bullet. He stopped at this evident hint, and, taking his dispatch bag from his shoulder, placed it significantly upon a boulder, and looked around as if to await the appearance of the unseen marksman. The rifle shot rang out again, the bag quivered, and turned over with a bullet hole through it!

He took out his white handkerchief and waved it. Another shot followed, and the handkerchief was snapped from his fingers, torn from corner to corner. A feeling of desperation and fury seized him; he was being played with by a masked and skillful assassin, who only waited until it pleased him to fire the deadly shot! But this time he could see the rifle smoke drifting from under a sycamore not a hundred yards away. He set his white lips together, but with a determined face and unfaltering step walked directly towards it. In another moment he believed and almost hoped that all would be over. With such a marksman he would not be maimed, but killed outright.

He had not covered half the distance before a man lounged out from behind the tree carelessly shouldering his rifle. He was tall but slightly built, with an amused, critical manner, and nothing about him to suggest the bloodthirsty assassin. He met Brice halfway, dropping his rifle slantingly across his breast with his hands lightly grasping the lock, and gazed at the young man curiously.

"You look as if you'd had a big scare, old man, but you've clear grit for all that!" he said, with a critical and reassuring smile. "Now, what are you doing here? Stay," he continued, as Brice's parched lips prevented him from replying immediately. "I ought to know your face. Hello! you're the expressman!" His glance suddenly shifted, and swept past Brice over the ground beyond him to the entrance of the hollow, but his smile returned as he apparently satisfied himself that the young man was alone. "Well, what do you want?"

"I want to see Snapshot Harry," said Brice, with an effort. His voice came back more slowly than his color, but that was perhaps hurried by a sense of shame at his physical weakness.

"What you want is a drop o' whiskey," said the stranger good humoredly, taking his arm, "and we'll find it in that shanty just behind the tree." To Brice's surprise, a few steps in that direction revealed a fair-sized cabin, with a slight pretentiousness about it of neatness, comfort, and picturesque effect, far superior to the Tarbox shanty. A few flowers were in boxes on the window—signs, as Brice fancied, of feminine taste. When they reached the threshold, somewhat of this quality was also visible in the interior. When Brice had partaken of the whiskey, the stranger, who had kept silence, pointed to a chair, and said smilingly:—

"I am Henry Dimwood, alias Snapshot Harry, and this is my house."

"I came to speak with you about the robbery of greenbacks from the coach last night," began Brice hurriedly, with a sudden access of hope at his reception.

an hour after a stage is stopped we have that road patrolled, every foot of it. While I was opening the box in the brush, the two fools, sneaking along the road, came slap upon one of my patrols, and then tried to run for it. One was dropped, but before he was plugged full of holes and hung up on a tree, he confessed, and said the other man who escaped had the greenbacks."

Brice's face fell. "Then they are lost," he said bitterly.

"Not unless he eats them—as he may want to do before I'm done on him, for he must either starve or come out. That road is still watched by my men from Tarbox's cabin to the bridge. He's there somewhere, and can't get forward or backward. Look!" he said, rising and going to the door. "That road," he pointed to the stage road,—a narrow ledge flanked on one side by a precipitous mountain wall, and on the other by an equally precipitate descent,—"is his limit and tether, and he can't escape on either side."

"But the trail?"

"There is but one entrance to it,—the way you came, and that is guarded too. From the time you entered it until you reached the bottom, you were signaled here from point to point! *He* would have been dropped! I merely gave *you* a hint of what might have happened to you, if you were up to any little game! You took it like a white man. Come, now! What is your business?"

Thus challenged, Brice plunged with youthful hopefulness into his plan; if, as he voiced it, it seemed to him a little extravagant, he was buoyed up by the frankness of the highwayman, who also had treated the double robbery with a levity that seemed almost as extravagant. He suggested that they should work together to recover the money; that the express company should know that the unprecedented stealthy introduction of robbers in the guise of passengers was not Snapshot Harry's method, and he repudiated it as unmanly and unsportsmanlike; and that, by using his superior skill and knowledge of the locality to recover the money and deliver the culprit into the company's hands, he would not only earn the reward that they should offer, but that he would evoke a sentiment that all Californians would understand and respect. The highwayman listened with a tolerant smile, but, to Brice's surprise, this appeal to his vanity touched him less than the prospective punishment of the thief.

"It would serve the d—d hound right," he muttered, "if, instead of being shot like a man, he was made to 'do time' in prison, like the ordinary sneak thief that he is." When Brice had concluded, he said briefly, "The only trouble with your plans, my young friend, is that about twenty-five men have got to consider them, and have *their* say about it. Every man in my gang is a shareholder in these greenbacks, for I work on the square; and it's for him to say whether he'll give them up for a reward and the good opinion of the express company. Perhaps," he went on, with a peculiar smile, "it's just as well that you tried it on me first! However, I'll sound the boys, and see what comes of it, but not until you're safe off the premises."

"And you'll let me assist you?" said Brice eagerly.

Snapshot Harry smiled again. "Well, if you come across the d—d thief, and you recognize him and can get the greenbacks from him, I'll pass over the game to you." He rose and added, apparently by way of fare-well, "Perhaps it's just as well that I should give you a guide part of the way to prevent accidents." He went to a door leading to an adjoining room, and called "Flo!"

Brice's heart leaped! If he had forgotten her in the excitement of his interview, he atoned for it by a vivid blush. Her own color was a little heightened as she slipped into the room, but the two managed to look demurely at each other, without a word of recognition.

"This is my niece, Flora," said Snapshot Harry, with a slight wave of the hand that was by no means uncourtly, "and her company will keep you from any impertinent questioning as well as if I were with you. This is Mr. Brice, Flo, who came to see me on busi-ness, and has quite forgotten my practical joking."

The girl acknowledged Brice's bow with a shyness very different from her manner of the evening before. Brice felt embarrassed and evidently showed it, for his host, with a smile, put an end to the constraint by shaking the young man's hand heartily, bidding him good-by, and accompanying him to the door.

Once on their way, Mr. Brice's spirits returned. "I told you last night," he said, "that I hoped to meet you the next time with a better introduction. You sug-gested your uncle's. Well, are you satisfied?"

"But you didn't come to see *me*," said the girl mischievously.

"How do you know what my intentions were?" returned the young man gayly, gazing at the girl's charming face with a serious doubt as to the singleness of his own intentions.

"Oh, because I know," she answered, with a toss of her brown head. "I heard what you said to uncle Harry."

Mr. Brice's brow contracted. "Perhaps you saw me, too, when I came," he said, with a slight touch of bitterness as he thought of his reception.

Miss Flo laughed. Brice walked on silently; the girl was heartless and worthy of her education. After a pause she said demurely, "I knew he wouldn't hurt you—but *you* didn't. That's where you showed your grit in walking straight on."

"And I suppose you were greatly amused," he replied scornfully.

The girl lifted her arms a little wearily, as with a half sigh she readjusted her brown braids under her uncle's gray slouch hat, which she had caught up as she passed out. "Thar ain't much to laugh at here!" she said. "But it was mighty funny when you tried to put your hat straight, and then found thur was that bullet hole right through the brim! And the way you stared at it—Lordy!"

Her musical laugh was infectious, and swept away his outraged dignity. He laughed too. At last she said, gazing at his hat, "It won't do for you to go back to your folks wearin' that sort o' thing. Here! Take mine!" With a saucy movement she audaciously lifted his hat from his head, and placed her own upon it.

"But this is your uncle's hat," he remonstrated.

"All the same; he spoiled yours," she laughed, adjusting his hat upon her own head. "But I'll keep yours to remember you by. I'll loop it up by this hole, and it'll look mighty purty. Jes' see!" She plucked a wild rose from a bush by the wayside, and, passing the stalk through the bullet hole, pinned the brim against the crown by a thorn. "There," she said, putting on the hat again with a little affectation of coquetry, "how's that?"

Mr. Brice thought it very picturesque and becoming to the graceful head and laughing eyes beneath it, and said so. Then, becoming in his turn audacious, he drew nearer to her side.

"I suppose you know the forfeit of putting on a gentleman's hat?"

Apparently she did, for she suddenly made a warning gesture, and said, "Not here! It would be a bigger forfeit than you'd keer fo'." Before he could reply she turned aside as if quite innocently, and passed into the shade of a fringe of buckeyes. He followed quickly. "I didn't mean that," she said; but in the mean time he had kissed the pink tip of her ear under its brown coils. He was, nevertheless, somewhat discomfited by her undisturbed manner and serene face. "Ye don't seem to mind bein' shot at," she said, with an odd smile, "but it won't do for you to kalkilate that *everybody* shoots as keerfully as uncle Harry."

"I don't understand," he replied, struck by her manner.

"Ye ain't very complimentary, or you'd allow that other folks might be wantin' what you took just now, and might consider you was poachin'," she returned gravely. "My best and strongest holt among those men is that uncle Harry would kill the first one who tried anything like that on—and they know it. That's how I get all the liberty I want here, and can come and go alone as I like."

Brice's face flushed quickly with genuine shame and remorse. "Do forgive me," he said hurriedly. "I didn't think—I'm a brute and a fool!"

"Uncle Harry allowed you was either drunk or a born idiot when you was promenadin' into the valley just now," she said, with a smile.

"And what did you think?" he asked a little uneasily.

"I thought you didn't look like a drinkin' man," she answered audaciously.

Brice bit his lip and walked on silently, at which she cast a sidelong glance under her widely spaced heavy lashes and said demurely, "I thought last night it was mighty good for you to stand up for your frien' Yuba Bill, and then, after ye knew who I was, to let the folks see you kinder cottoned to me too. Not in the style o' that land-grabber Heckshill, nor that peart newspaper man, neither. Of course I gave them as good as they sent," she went on, with a little laugh, but Brice could see that her sensitive lip in profile had the tremulous and resentful curve of one who was accustomed to

44

slight and annoyance. Was it possible that this reck-less, self-contained girl felt her position keenly?

"I am proud to have your good opinion," he said, with a certain respect mingled with his admiring glance, "even if I have not your uncle's."

"Oh, he likes you well enough, or he wouldn't have hearkened to you a minute," she said quickly. "When you opened out about them greenbacks, I jes' clutched my cheer *so*," she illustrated her words with a gesture of her hands, and her face actually seemed to grow pale at the recollection,—"and I nigh started up to stop ye; but that idea of Yuba Bill bein' robbed *twice i* think tickled him awful. But it was lucky none o' the gang heard ye or suspected anything. I reckon that's why he sent me with you,—to keep them from doggin' you and askin' questions that a straight man like you would be sure to answer. But they daren't come nigh ye as long as I'm with you!" She threw back her head and rose-crested hat with a mock air of protection that, however, had a certain real pride in it.

"I am very glad of that, if it gives me the chance of having your company alone," returned Brice, smil-ing, "and very grateful to your uncle, whatever were his reasons for making you my guide. But you have already been that to me," and he told her of the foot-prints. "But for you," he added, with gentle signifi-cance, "I should not have been here."

She was silent for a moment, and he could only see the back of her head and its heavy brown coils.

After a pause she asked abruptly, "Where's your handkerchief?"

He took it from his pocket; her ingenious uncle's bullet had torn rather than pierced the cambric.

"I thought so," she said, gravely examining it, "but I kin mend it as good as new. I reckon you allow I can't sew," she continued, "but I do heaps of mendin', as the digger squaw and Chinamen we have here do only the coarser work. I'll send it back to you, and meanwhiles you keep mine."

She drew a handkerchief from her pocket and handed it to him. To his great surprise it was a delicate one, beautifully embroidered, and utterly incongruous to her station. The idea that flashed upon him, it is to be feared, showed itself momentarily in his hesitation and embarrassment.

She gave a quick laugh. "Don't be frightened. It's bought and paid for. Uncle Harry don't touch passengers' fixin's; that ain't his style. You oughter know that." Yet in spite of her laugh, he could see the sensitive pout of her lower lip.

"I was only thinking," he said hurriedly and sympathetically, "that it was too fine for me. But I will be proud to keep it as a souvenir of you. It's not too pretty for *that*!"

"Uncle gets me these things. He don't keer what they cost," she went on, ignoring the compliment. "Why, I've got awfully fine gowns up there that I only wear when I go to Marysville oncet in a while."

"Does he take you there?" asked Brice.

"No!" she answered quietly. "Not"—a little defiantly—"that he's afeard, for they can't prove anything against him; no man kin swear to him, and thar ain't an officer that keers to go for him. But he's that shy for *me* he don't keer to have me mixed with him."

"But nobody recognizes you?"

"Sometimes—but I don't keer for that." She cocked her hat a little audaciously, but Brice noticed that her arms afterwards dropped at her side with the same weary gesture he had observed before. "Whenever I go into shops it's always 'Yes, miss,' and 'No, miss,' and 'Certainly, Miss Dimwood.' Oh, they're mighty respectful. I reckon they allow that Snapshot Harry's rifle carries far."

Presently she faced him again, for their conversation had been carried on in profile. There was a critical, searching look in her brown eyes.

"Here I'm talkin' to you as if you were one"—Mr. Brice was positive she was going to say "one of the gang," but she hesitated and concluded, "one of my relations—like cousin Hiram."

"I wish you would think of me as being as true a friend," said the young man earnestly.

She did not reply immediately, but seemed to be examining the distance. They were not far from the canyon now, and the river bank. A fringe of buckeyes hid the base of the mountain, which had begun to tower up above them to the invisible stage road overhead. "I am going to be a real guide to you now," she said suddenly. "When we reach that buckeye corner and are out of sight, we will turn into it instead of going through the canyon. You shall go up the mountain to the stage road, from *this* side."

"But it is impossible!" he exclaimed, in astonishment. "Your uncle said so."

"Coming *down*, but not going up," she returned, with a laugh. "I found it, and no one knows it but myself."

He glanced up at the towering cliff; its nearly perpendicular flanks were seamed with fissures, some clefts deeply set with stunted growths of thorn and "scrub," but still sheer and forbidding, and then glanced back at her incredulously. "I will show you," she said, answering his look with a smile of triumph. "I haven't tramped over this whole valley for nothing! But wait until we reach the river bank. They must think that we've gone through the canyon."

"They?

"Yes—any one who is watching us," said the girl dryly.

A few steps further on brought them to the buckeye thicket, which extended to the river bank and mouth of the canyon. The girl lingered for a moment ostentatiously before it, and then, saying "Come," suddenly turned at right angles into the thicket. Brice followed, and the next moment they were hidden by its friendly screen from the valley. On the other side rose the mountain wall, leaving a narrow trail before them. It was composed of the rocky debris and fallen trees of the cliff, from which buckeyes and larches were now springing. It was uneven, irregular, and slowly ascending; but the young girl led the way with the free footstep of a mountaineer, and yet a grace that was akin to delicacy. Nor could he fail to notice that, after the Western girl's fashion, she was shod more elegantly and lightly than was consistent with the rude and rustic surroundings. It was the same slim shoe-print which had guided him that morning. Presently she stopped, and seemed to be gazing curiously at the cliff side. Brice followed the direction of her eyes. On a protruding bush at the edge of one of the wooded clefts of the mountain flank something was hanging, and in the freshening southerly wind was flapping heavily, like a raven's wing, or as if still saturated with the last night's rain. "That's mighty queer!" said Flo, gazing intently at the unsightly and incongruous attachment to the shrub, which had a vague, weird suggestion. "It wasn't there yesterday."

"It looks like a man's coat," remarked Brice uneasily.

"Whew!" said the girl. "Then somebody has come down who won't go up again! There's a lot of fresh rocks and brush here, too. What's that?" She was pointing to a spot some yards before them where there had been a recent precipitation of debris and uprooted shrubs. But mingled with it lay a mass of rags strangely akin to the tattered remnant that flagged from the bush a hundred feet above them. The girl suddenly uttered a sharp feminine cry of mingled horror and disgust,—the first weakness of sex she had shown,— and, recoiling, grasped Brice's arm. "Don't go there! Come away!"

But Brice had already seen that which, while it shocked him, was urging him forward with an invincible fascination. Gently releasing himself, and bidding the girl stand back, he moved toward the unsightly heap. Gradually it disclosed a grotesque caricature of a human figure, but so maimed and doubled up that it seemed a stuffed and fallen scarecrow. As is common in men stricken suddenly down by accident in the fullness of life, the clothes asserted themselves before all else with a hideous ludicrousness, obliterating even the majesty of death in their helpless yet ironical incongruity. The garments seemed to have never fitted the wearer, but to have been assumed in ghastly jocularity,—a boot half off the swollen foot, a ripped waistcoat thrown over the shoulder, were like the properties of some low comedian. At first the body appeared to be headless; but as Brice cleared away the debris and lifted it, he saw with horror that the head was twisted under the shoulder, and swung helplessly from the dislocated neck. But that horror gave way to a more intense and thrilling emotion as he saw the face—although strangely free from laceration or disfigurement, and impurpled and distended into the simulation of a self-complacent smile—was a face he recognized! It was the face of the cynical traveler in the coach—the man who he was now satisfied had robbed it.

A strange and selfish resentment took possession of him. Here was the man through whom he had suffered shame and peril, and who even now seemed complacently victorious in death. He examined him closely; his coat and waistcoat had been partly torn away in his fall; his shirt still clung to him, but through its torn front could be seen a heavy treasure belt encircling his waist. Forgetting his disgust, Brice tore away the shirt and unloosed the belt. It was saturated with water like the rest of the clothing, but its pocket seemed heavy and distended. In another instant he had opened it, and discovered the envelope containing the packet of greenbacks, its seal still inviolate and unbroken. It was the stolen treasure!

A faint sigh recalled him to himself. The girl was standing a few feet from him, regarding him curiously.

"It's the thief himself!" he said, in a breathless explanation. "In trying to escape he must have fallen from the road above. But here are the greenbacks safe! We must go back to your uncle at once," he said excitedly. "Come!"

"Are you mad?" she cried, in astonishment.

"No," returned Brice, in equal astonishment, "but you know I agreed with him that we should work together to recover the money, and I must show him our good luck."

"He told you that if you met the thief and could get the money from him, you were welcome to it," said the girl gravely, "and you *have* got it."

"But not in the way he meant," returned Brice hurriedly. "This man's death is the result of his attempting to escape from your uncle's guards along the road; the merit of it belongs to them and your uncle. It would be cowardly and mean of me to take advantage of it."

The girl looked at him with an expression of mingled admiration and pity. "But the guards were placed there before he ever saw you," said she impatiently. "And whatever uncle Harry may want to do, he must do what the gang says. And with the money once in their possession, or even in yours, if they knew it, I wouldn't give much for its chances—or *yours* either—for gettin' out o' this hollow again."

"But if *they* are treacherous, that is no reason why I should be so," protested Brice stoutly.

"You've no right to say they were treacherous when they knew nothing of your plans," said the girl sharply. "Your company would have more call to say *you* were treacherous to it for making a plan without consultin' them." Brice winced, for he had never thought of that before. "You can offer that reward *after* you get away from here with the greenbacks. But," she added proudly, with a toss of her head, "go back if you want to! Tell him all! Tell him where you found it—tell him I did not take you through the canyon, but was showin' you a new trail I had never shown to *them*! Tell him that I am a traitor, for I have given them and him away to you, a stranger, and that you consider yourself the only straight and honest one about here!"

Brice flushed with shame. "Forgive me," he said hurriedly; "you are right and I am wrong again. I will do just what you say. I will first place these greenbacks in a secure place—and then"—

"Get away first—that's your only holt," she interrupted him quickly, her eyes still flashing through indignant tears. "Come quick, for I must put you on the trail before they miss me."

She darted forward; he followed, but she kept the lead, as much, he fancied, to evade his observation as to expedite his going. Presently they stopped before the sloping trunk of a huge pine that had long since fallen from the height above, but, although splintered where it had broken ground, had preserved some fifty feet of its straight trunk erect and leaning like a ladder against the mountain wall. "There," she said, hurriedly pointing to its decaying but still projecting lateral branches, "you climb it—I have. At the top you'll find it's stuck in a cleft among the brush. There's a little hollow and an old waterway from a spring above which makes a trail through the brush. It's as good as the trail you took from the stage road this mornin', but it's not as safe comin' down. Keep along it to the spring, and it will land ye jest the other side of uncle Hiram's cabin. Go quick! I'll wait here until ye've reached the cleft."

"But you," he said, turning toward her, "how can I ever thank you?"

As if anticipating a leave-taking, the girl had already withdrawn herself a few yards away, and simply made an upward gesture with her hand. "Quick! Up with you! Every minute now is a risk to me."

Thus appealed to, Brice could only comply. Perhaps he was a little hurt at the girl's evident desire to avoid a gentler parting. Securing his prized envelope within his breast, he began to ascend the tree. Its inclination, and the aid offered by the broken stumps of branches, made this comparatively easy, and in a few moments he reached its top, and stood upon a little ledge in the wall. A swift glance around him revealed the whole waterway or fissure slanting upward along the mountain face. Then he turned quickly to look down the dizzy height. At first he could distinguish nothing but the top of the buckeyes and their white clustering blossoms. Then something fluttered,—the torn white handkerchief of his that she had kept. And then he caught a single glimpse of the flower-plumed hat receding rapidly among the trees, and Flora Dimwood was gone.

III

In twenty-four hours Edward Brice was in San Francisco. But although successful and the bearer of the treasure, it is doubtful if he approached this end of his journey with the temerity he had shown on entering the robbers' valley. A consciousness that the methods he had employed might excite the ridicule, if not the censure, of his principals, or that he might have compromised them in his meeting with Snapshot Harry, considerably modified his youthful exultation. It is possible that Flora's reproach, which still rankled in his mind, may have quickened his sensitiveness on that point. However, he had resolved to tell the whole truth, except his episode with Flora, and to place the conduct of Snapshot Harry and the Tarboxes in as favorable a light as possible. But first he had recourse to the manager, a man of shrewd worldly experience, who had recommended him to his place. When he had finished and handed him the treasured envelope, the man looked at him with a critical and yet not unkindly expression. "Perhaps it's just as well, Brice, that you did come to me at first, and did not make your report to the president and directors."

"I suppose," said Brice diffidently, "that they wouldn't have liked my communicating with the highwayman without their knowledge?"

"More than that—they wouldn't have believed your story."

"Not believe it?" cried Brice, flushing quickly. "Do you think"—

The manager checked him with a laugh. "Hold on! I believe every word of it, and why? Because you've added nothing to it to make yourself the regular hero. Why, with your opportunity, and no one able to contradict you, you might have told me you had a hand-to-hand fight with the thief, and had to kill him to recover the money, and even brought your handkerchief and hat back with the bullet holes to prove it." Brice winked as he thought of the fair possessor of those articles. "But as a story for general circulation, it won't do. Have you told it to any one else? Does any one know what happened but yourself?"

Brice thought of Flora, but he had resolved not to compromise her, and he had a consciousness that she would be equally loyal to him. "No one," he answered boldly.

"Very good. And I suppose you wouldn't mind if it were kept out of the newspapers? You're not hankering after a reputation as a hero?"

"Certainly not," said Brice indignantly.

"Well, then, we'll keep it where it is. You will say nothing. I will hand over the greenbacks to the company, but only as much of your story as I think they'll stand. You're all right as it is. Yuba Bill has already set you up in his report to the company, and the recovery of this money will put you higher! Only, the *public* need know nothing about it."

"But," asked Brice amazedly, "how can it be prevented? The shippers who lost the money will have to know that it has been recovered."

"Why should they? The company will assume the risk, and repay them just the same. It's a great deal better to have the reputation for accepting the responsibility than for the shippers to think that they only get their money through the accident of its recovery."

Brice gasped at this large business truth. Besides, it occurred to him that it kept the secret, and Flora's participation in it, from Snapshot Harry and the gang. He had not thought of that before.

"Come," continued the manager, with official curtness. "What do you say? Are you willing to leave it to me?"

Brice hesitated a moment. It was not what his impulsive truthful nature had suggested. It was not what his youthful fancy had imagined. He had not worked upon the sympathies of the company on behalf of Snapshot Harry as he believed he would do. He had not even impressed the manager. His story, far from exciting a chivalrous sentiment, had been pronounced improbable. Yet he reflected he had so far protected *her*, and he consented with a sigh.

Nevertheless, the result ought to have satisfied him. A dazzling check, inclosed in a letter of thanks from the company the next day, and his promotion from "the road" to the San Francisco office, would have been quite enough for any one but Edward Brice. Yet he was grateful, albeit a little frightened and remorseful over his luck. He could not help thinking of the kindly tolerance of the highwayman, the miserable death of the actual thief, which had proved his own salvation, and above all the generous, high-spirited girl who had aided his escape. While on his way to San Francisco, and yet in the first glow of his success, he had written her a few lines from Marysville, inclosed in a letter to Mr. Tarbox. He had received no reply.

Then a week passed. He wrote again, and still no reply. Then a vague feeling of jealousy took possession of him as he remembered her warning hint of the attentions to which she was subjected, and he became singularly appreciative of Snapshot Harry's proficiency as a marksman. Then, cruelest of all, for your impassioned lover is no lover at all if not cruel in his imaginings, he remembered how she had evaded her uncle's espionage with *him*; could she not equally with *another?* Perhaps that was why she had hurried him away,—why she had prevented his returning to her uncle. Following this came another week of disappointment and equally miserable cynical philosophy, in which he persuaded himself he was perfectly satisfied with his material advancement, that it was the only outcome of his adventure to be recognized; and he was more miserable than ever.

A month had passed, when one morning he received a small package by post. The address was in a handwriting unknown to him, but opening the parcel he was surprised to find only a handkerchief neatly folded. Examining it closely, he found it was his own,—the one he had given her, the rent made by her uncle's bullet so ingeniously and delicately mended as to almost simulate embroidery. The joy that suddenly filled him at this proof of her remembrance showed him too plainly how hollow had been his cynicism and how lasting his hope! Turning over the wrapper eagerly, he discovered what he had at first thought was some business card. It was, indeed, printed and not engraved, in some common newspaper type, and bore the address, "Hiram Tarbox, Land and Timber Agent, 1101 California Street." He again examined the parcel; there was nothing else,—not a line from *her*! But it was a clue at last, and she had not forgotten him! He seized his hat, and ten minutes later was breasting the steep sand hill into which California

Street in those days plunged, and again emerged at its crest, with a few struggling houses.

But when he reached the summit he could see that the outline of the street was still plainly marked along the distance by cottages and new suburban villa-like blocks of houses. No. 1101 was in one of these blocks, a small tenement enough, but a palace compared to Mr. Tarbox's Sierran cabin. He impetuously rang the bell, and without waiting to be announced dashed into the little drawing-room and Mr. Tarbox's presence. That had changed too; Mr. Tarbox was arrayed in a suit of clothes as new, as cheaply decorative, as fresh and, apparently, as damp as his own drawing room.

"Did you get my letter? Did you give her the one I inclosed? Why didn't you answer?" burst out Brice, after his first breathless greeting.

Mr. Tarbox's face here changed so suddenly into his old dejected doggedness that Brice could have imagined himself back in the Sierran cabin. The man straightened and bowed himself at Brice's questions, and then replied with bold, deliberate emphasis:

"Yes, I *did* get your letter. *I didn't* give no letter o' yours to her. And I didn't answer your letter *before*, for I didn't propose to answer it *at all*."

"Why?" demanded Brice indignantly.

"I didn't give her your letter because I didn't kalkilate to be any go-between 'twixt you and Snapshot Harry's niece. Look yar, Mr. Brice. Sense I read that 'ar paragraph in that paper you gave me, I allowed to myself that it wasn't the square thing for me to have any more doin's with him, and I quit it. I jest chucked your letter in the fire. I didn't answer you because I reckoned I'd no call to correspond with ye, and when I showed ye that trail over to Harry's camp, it was ended. I've got a house and business to look arter, and it don't jibe with keepin' company with 'road agents.' That's what I got outer that paper you gave me, Mr. Brice."

Rage and disgust filled Brice at the man's utter selfishness and shameless desertion of his kindred, none the less powerfully that he remembered the part he himself had played in concocting the paragraph. "Do you mean to say," he demanded passionately, "that for the sake of that foolish paragraph you gave up your own kindred? That you truckled to the mean prejudices of your neighbors and kept that poor, defenseless girl from the only honest roof she could find refuge under? That you dared to destroy my letter to her, and made her believe I was as selfish and ungrateful as yourself?"

"Young feller," said Mr. Tarbox still more deliberately, yet with a certain dignity that Brice had never noticed before, "what's between you and Flo, and what rights she has fer thinkin' ye 'ez selfish' and 'ez ongrateful' ez me—ef she does, I dunno!—but when ye talk o' me givin' up my kindred, and sling such hogwash ez 'ongrateful' and 'selfish' round this yer sittin'-room, mebbe it mout occur to ye that Harry Dimwood might hev *his* opinion o' what was 'ongrateful' and 'selfish' ef I'd played in between his niece and a young man o' the express company, his nat'ral en-emy. It's one thing to hev helped ye to see her in her uncle's own camp, but another to help ye by makin' a clandecent post-offis o' my cabin. Ef, instead o' writin', you'd hev posted yourself by comin' to me, you mout hev found out that when I broke with Harry I offered to take Flo with me for good and all—ef he'd keep away from us. And that's the kind o' 'honest roof' that that thar 'poor defenseless girl' got under when her crippled mother died three weeks ago, and left Harry free. It was by 'trucklin'' to them 'mean prejudices,' and readin' that thar 'foolish paragraph,' that I settled this thing then and thar!"

Brice's revulsion of sentiment was so complete, and the gratitude that beamed in his eyes was so sincere, that Mr. Tarbox hardly needed the profuse apologies which broke from him. "Forgive me!" he continued to stammer, "I have wronged you, wronged *her*—every-body. But as you know, Mr. Tarbox, how I have felt over this, how deeply—how passionately"—

"It *does* make a man loony sometimes," said Mr. Tar-box, relaxing into demure dryness again, "so I reckon you *did*! Mebbe she reckoned so, too, for she asked me to give you the handkercher I sent ye. It looked as if she'd bin doin' some fancy work on it."

Brice glanced quickly at Mr. Tarbox's face. It was stolid and imperturbable. She had evidently kept the secret of what passed in the hollow to herself. For the first time he looked around the room curiously. "I didn't know you were a land agent before," he said.

"No more I was! All that kem out o' that paragraph, Mr. Brice. That man Heckshill, who was so mighty perlite that night, wrote to me afterwards that he didn't know my name till he'd seed that paragraph, and he wanted to know ef, ez a 'well-known citizen,' I could recommend him some timber lands. I recommended him half o' my own quarter section, and he took it. He's puttin' up a mill thar, and that's another reason why we want peace and quietness up thar. I'm tryin' (betwixt and between us, Mr. Brice) to get Harry to cl'ar out and sell his rights in the valley and the water power on the Fork to Heckshill and me. I'm opening a business here."

"Then you've left Mrs. Tarbox with Miss Flora in your cabin while you attend to business here," said Brice tentatively.

"Not exactly, Mr. Brice. The old woman thought it a good chance to come to 'Frisco and put Flo in one o' them Catholic convent schools—that asks no questions whar the raw logs come from, and turns 'em out first-class plank all round. You foller me, Mr. Brice? But Mrs. Tarbox is jest in the next room, and would admire to tell ye all this—and I'll go in and send her to you." And with a patronizing wave of the hand, Mr. Tarbox complacently disappeared in the hall.

Mr. Brice was not sorry to be left to himself in his utter bewilderment! Flo, separated from her detrimental uncle, and placed in a convent school! Tarbox, the obscure pioneer, a shrewd speculator emerging into success, and taking the uncle's place! And all this within that month which he had wasted with absurd repinings. How feeble seemed his own adventure and advancement; how even ludicrous his pretensions to any patronage and superiority. How this common backwoodsman had set him in his place as easily as *she* had evaded the advances of the journalist and Heck-shill! They had taught him a lesson; perhaps even the sending back of his handkerchief was part of it! His heart grew heavy; he walked to the window and gazed out with a long sigh.

A light laugh, that might have been an echo of the one which had attracted him that night in Tarbox's cabin, fell upon his ear. He turned quickly to meet Flora Dimwood's laughing eyes shining upon him as she stood in the doorway.

Many a time during that month he had thought of this meeting—had imagined what it would be like— what would be his manner towards her—what would be her greeting, and what they would say. He would be cold, gentle, formal, gallant, gay, sad, trustful, re-proachful, even as the moods in which he thought of her came to his foolish brain. He would always begin with respectful seriousness, or a frankness equal to her own, but never, never again would he offend as he had offended under the buckeyes! And now, with her pretty face shining upon him, all his plans, his speeches, his preparations vanished, and left him dumb. Yet he moved towards her with a brief artic-ulate something on his lips,—something between a laugh and a sigh,—but that really was a kiss, and—in point of fact—promptly folded her in his arms.

Yet it was certainly direct, and perhaps the best that could be done, for the young lady did not emerge from it as coolly, as unemotionally, nor possibly as quickly as she had under the shade of the buckeyes. But she persuaded him—by still holding his hand— to sit beside her on the chilly, highly varnished "green rep" sofa, albeit to him it was a bank in a bower of enchantment. Then she said, with adorable reproach- fulness, "You don't ask what I did with the body."

Mr. Edward Brice started. He was young, and un- familiar with the evasive expansiveness of the female mind at such supreme moments.

"The body—oh, yes—certainly."

"I buried it myself—it was suthin too awful!—and the gang would have been sure to have found it, and the empty belt. I burned *that*. So that nobody knows nothin'."

It was not a time for strictly grammatical negatives, and I am afraid that the girl's characteristically fa- miliar speech, even when pathetically corrected here and there by the influence of the convent, endeared her the more to him. And when she said, "And now, Mr. Edward Brice, sit over at that end of the sofy and let's talk," they talked. They talked for an hour, more or less continuously, until they were surprised by a discreet cough and the entrance of Mrs. Tarbox. Then there was more talk, and the discovery that Mr. Brice was long due at the office.

"Ye might drop in, now and then, whenever ye feel like it, and Flo is at home," suggested Mrs. Tarbox at parting.

Mr. Brice *did* drop in frequently during the next month. On one of these occasions Mr. Tarbox accompanied him to the door. "And now—ez everything is settled and in order, Mr. Brice, and ef you should be wantin' to say anything about it to your bosses at the office, ye may mention *my* name ez Flo Dimwood's second cousin, and say I'm a depositor in their bank. And," with greater deliberation, "ef anything at any time should be thrown up at ye for marryin' a niece o' Snapshot Harry's, ye might mention, keerless like, that Snapshot Harry, under the name o' Henry J. Dimwood, has held shares in their old bank for years!"

A Treasure of the Redwoods

PART I

Mr. Jack Fleming stopped suddenly before a life-less and decaying redwood-tree with an expression of disgust and impatience. It was the very tree he had passed only an hour before, and he now knew he had been describing that mysterious and hopeless circle familiar enough to those lost in the woods.

There was no mistaking the tree, with its one broken branch which depended at an angle like the arm of a semaphore; nor did it relieve his mind to reflect that his mishap was partly due to his own foolish abstraction. He was returning to camp from a neighboring mining town, and while indulging in the usual daydreams of a youthful prospector, had deviated from his path in attempting to make a short cut through the forest. He had lost the sun, his only guide, in the thickly interlaced boughs above him, which suffused though the long columnar vault only a vague, melancholy twilight. He had evidently penetrated some unknown seclusion, absolutely primeval and untrodden. The thick layers of decaying bark and the desiccated dust of ages deadened his footfall and invested the gloom with a profound silence.

As he stood for a moment or two, irresolute, his ear, by this time attuned to the stillness, caught the faint but distinct lap and trickle of water. He was hot and thirsty, and turned instinctively in that direction. A very few paces brought him to a fallen tree; at the foot of its upturned roots gurgled the spring whose upwelling stream had slowly but persistently loosened their hold on the soil, and worked their ruin. A pool of cool and clear water, formed by the disruption of the soil, overflowed, and after a few yards sank again in the sodden floor.

As he drank and bathed his head and hands in this sylvan basin, he noticed the white glitter of a quartz ledge in its depths, and was considerably surprised and relieved to find, hard by, an actual outcrop of that rock through the thick carpet of bark and dust. This betokened that he was near the edge of the forest or some rocky opening. He fancied that the light grew clearer beyond, and the presence of a few fronds of ferns confirmed him in the belief that he was approaching a different belt of vegetation. Presently he saw the vertical beams of the sun again piercing the opening in the distance. With this prospect of speedy deliverance from the forest at last secure, he did not hurry forward, but on the contrary coolly retraced his footsteps to the spring again. The fact was that the instincts and hopes of the prospector were strongly dominant in him, and having noticed the quartz ledge and the contiguous outcrop, he determined to examine them more closely. He had still time to find his way home, and it might not be so easy to penetrate the wilderness again. Unfortunately, he had neither pick, pan, nor shovel with him, but a very cursory displacement of the soil around the spring and at the outcrop with his hands showed him the usual red soil and decomposed quartz which constituted an "indication." Yet none knew better than himself how disappointing and illusive its results often were, and he regretted that he had not a pan to enable him to test the soil by washing it at the spring. If there were only a miner's cabin handy, he could easily borrow what he wanted. It was just the usual luck,—"the things a man sees when he hasn't his gun with him!"

He turned impatiently away again in the direction of the opening. When he reached it, he found himself on a rocky hillside sloping toward a small green valley. A light smoke curled above a clump of willows; it was from the chimney of a low dwelling, but a second glance told him that it was no miner's cabin. There was a larger clearing around the house, and some rude attempt at cultivation in a roughly fenced area. Nevertheless, he determined to try his luck in borrowing a pick and pan there; at the worst he could inquire his way to the main road again.

A hurried scramble down the hill brought him to the dwelling,—a rambling addition of sheds to the usual log cabin. But he was surprised to find that its exterior, and indeed the palings of the fence around it, were covered with the stretched and drying skins of animals. The pelts of bear, panther, wolf, and fox were intermingled with squirrel and wildcat skins, and the displayed wings of eagle, hawk, and kingfisher. There was no trail leading to or from the cabin; it seemed to have been lost in this opening of the encompassing woods and left alone and solitary.

The barking of a couple of tethered hounds at last brought a figure to the door of the nearest lean-to shed. It seemed to be that of a young girl, but it was clad in garments so ridiculously large and disproportionate that it was difficult to tell her precise age. A calico dress was pinned up at the skirt, and tightly girt at the waist by an apron—so long that one corner had to be tucked in at the apron string diagonally, to keep the wearer from treading on it. An enormous sunbonnet of yellow nankeen completely concealed her head and face, but allowed two knotted and twisted brown tails of hair to escape under its frilled cape behind. She was evidently engaged in some culinary work, and still held a large tin basin or pan she had been cleaning clasped to her breast.

Fleming's eye glanced at it covetously, ignoring the figure behind it. But he was diplomatic.

"I have lost my way in the woods. Can you tell me in what direction the main road lies?"

She pointed a small red hand apparently in the direction he had come. "Straight over thar—across the hill."

Fleming sighed. He had been making a circuit of the forest instead of going through it—and this open space containing the cabin was on a remote outskirt!

"How far is it to the road?" he asked.

"Jest a spell arter ye rise the hill, ef ye keep 'longside the woods. But it's a right smart chance beyond, ef ye go through it."

This was quite plain to him. In the local dialect a "spell" was under a mile; "a right smart chance" might be three or four miles farther. Luckily the spring and outcrop were near the outskirts; he would pass near them again on his way. He looked longingly at the pan which she still held in her hands. "Would you mind lending me that pan for a little while?" he said half laughingly.

"Wot for?" demanded the girl quickly. Yet her tone was one of childish curiosity rather than suspicion. Fleming would have liked to avoid the question and the consequent exposure of his discovery which a direct answer implied. But he saw it was too late now.

"I want to wash a little dirt," he said bluntly.

The girl turned her deep sunbonnet toward him. Somewhere in its depths he saw the flash of white teeth. "Go along with ye—ye're funnin'!" she said.

"I want to wash out some dirt in that pan—I'm prospecting for gold," he said; "don't you understand?"

"Are ye a miner?"

"Well, yes—a sort of one," he returned, with a laugh.

"Then ye'd better be scootin' out o' this mighty quick

afore dad comes. He don't cotton to miners, and won't have 'em around. That's why he lives out here."

"Well, I don't live out here," responded the young man lightly. "I shouldn't be here if I hadn't lost my way, and in half an hour I'll be off again. So I'm not likely to bother him. But," he added, as the girl still hesitated, "I'll leave a deposit for the pan, if you like."

"Leave a which?"

"The money that the pan's worth," said Fleming impatiently.

The huge sunbonnet stiffly swung around like the wind-sail of a ship and stared at the horizon. "I don't want no money. Ye kin git," said the voice in its depths.

"Look here," he said desperately, "I only wanted to prove to you that I'll bring your pan back safe. Now look! If you don't like to take money, I'll leave this ring with you until I come back. There!" He slipped a small specimen ring, made out of his first gold findings, from his little finger.

The sunbonnet slowly swung around again and stared at the ring. Then the little red right hand reached forward, took the ring, placed it on the forefinger of the left hand, with all the other fingers widely extended for the sunbonnet to view, and all the while the pan was still held against her side by the other hand. Fleming noticed that the hands, though tawny and not over clean, were almost child-like in size, and that the forefinger was much too small for the ring. He tried to fathom the depths of the sun-bonnet, but it was dented on one side, and

71

he could discern only a single pale blue eye and a thin black arch of eyebrow.

"Well," said Fleming, "is it a go?"

"Of course ye'll be comin' back for it again," said the girl slowly.

There was so much of hopeless disappointment at that prospect in her voice that Fleming laughed outright. "I'm afraid I shall, for I value the ring very much," he said.

The girl handed him the pan. "It's our bread pan," she said.

It might have been anything, for it was by no means new; indeed, it was battered on one side and the bottom seemed to have been broken; but it would serve, and Fleming was anxious to be off. "Thank you," he said briefly, and turned away. The hound barked again as he passed; he heard the girl say, "Shut your head, Tige!" and saw her turn back into the kitchen, still holding the ring before the sunbonnet.

When he reached the woods, he attacked the outcrop he had noticed, and detached with his hands and the aid of a sharp rock enough of the loose soil to fill the pan. This he took to the spring, and, lowering the pan in the pool, began to wash out its contents with the centrifugal movement of the experienced prospector. The saturated red soil overflowed the brim with that liquid ooze known as "slumgullion," and turned the crystal pool to the color of blood until the soil was washed away. Then the smaller stones were carefully removed and examined, and then another washing of the now nearly empty pan showed the fine black sand covering the bottom. This was in turn as gently washed away.

Alas! the clean pan showed only one or two minute glistening yellow scales, like pinheads, adhering from their specific gravity to the bottom; gold, indeed, but merely enough to indicate "the color," and common to ordinary prospecting in his own locality.

He tried another panful with the same result. He became aware that the pan was leaky, and that infinite care alone prevented the bottom from falling out during the washing. Still it was an experiment, and the result a failure.

Fleming was too old a prospector to take his disappointment seriously. Indeed, it was characteristic of that performance and that period that failure left neither hopelessness nor loss of faith behind it; the prospector had simply miscalculated the exact locality, and was equally as ready to try his luck again. But Fleming thought it high time to return to his own mining work in camp, and at once set off to return the pan to its girlish owner and recover his ring.

As he approached the cabin again, he heard the sound of singing. It was evidently the girl's voice, uplifted in what seemed to be a fragment of some negro camp-meeting hymn:—

"Dar was a poor man and his name it was Lazarum,
Lord bress de Lamb—glory hallelugerum!
Lord bress de Lamb!"

The first two lines had a brisk movement, accented apparently by the clapping of hands or the beating of a tin pan, but the refrain, "Lord bress de Lamb," was drawn out in a lugubrious chant of infinite tenuity.

"The rich man died and he went straight to hellerum.
Lord bress de Lamb—glory hallelugerum!
Lord bress de Lamb!"

Fleming paused at the cabin door. Before he could rap the voice rose again:—

"When ye see a poo' man be sure to give him crumbsorum,
Lord bress de Lamb—glory hallelugerum!
Lord bress de Lamb!"

At the end of this interminable refrain, drawn out in a youthful nasal contralto, Fleming knocked. The girl instantly appeared, holding the ring in her fingers. "I reckoned it was you," she said, with an affected briskness, to conceal her evident dislike at parting with the trinket. "There it is!"

But Fleming was too astounded to speak. With the opening of the door the sunbonnet had fallen back like a buggy top, disclosing for the first time the head and shoulders of the wearer. She was not a child, but a smart young woman of seventeen or eighteen, and much of his embarrassment arose from the consciousness that he had no reason whatever for having believed her otherwise.

"I hope I didn't interrupt your singing," he said awkwardly.

"It was only one o' mammy's camp-meetin' songs," said the girl.

"Your mother? Is she in?" he asked, glancing past the girl into the kitchen.

"'Tain't mother—she's dead. Mammy's our old nurse. She's gone to Jimtown, and taken my duds to get some new ones fitted to me. These are some o' mother's."

This accounted for her strange appearance; but Fleming noticed that the girl's manner had not the slightest consciousness of their unbecomingness, nor of the charms of face and figure they had marred.

She looked at him curiously. "Hev you got religion?"

"Well, no!" said Fleming, laughing; "I'm afraid not."

"Dad hez—he's got it pow'ful."

"Is that the reason he don't like miners?" asked Fleming.

"'Take not to yourself the mammon of unrighteousness,'" said the girl, with the confident air of repeating a lesson. "That's what the Book says."

"But I read the Bible, too," replied the young man.

"Dad says, 'The letter killeth'!" said the girl sententiously.

Fleming looked at the trophies nailed on the walls with a vague wonder if this peculiar Scriptural destructiveness had anything to do with his skill as a marksman. The girl followed his eye.

"Dad's a mighty hunter afore the Lord."

"What does he do with these skins?"

"Trades 'em off for grub and fixin's. But he don't believe in trottin' round in the mud for gold."

"Don't you suppose these animals would have preferred it if he had? Gold hunting takes nothing from anybody."

The girl stared at him, and then, to his great surprise, laughed instead of being angry. It was a very fascinating laugh in her imperfectly nourished pale face, and her little teeth revealed the bluish milky whiteness of pips of young Indian corn.

"Wot yer lookin' at?" she asked frankly.

"You," he replied, with equal frankness.

"It's them duds," she said, looking down at her dress; "I reckon I ain't got the hang o' 'em."

Yet there was not the slightest tone of embarrassment or even coquetry in her manner, as with both hands she tried to gather in the loose folds around her waist.

"Let me help you," he said gravely.

She lifted up her arms with childlike simplicity and backed toward him as he stepped behind her, drew in the folds, and pinned them around what proved a very small waist indeed. Then he untied the apron, took it off, folded it in half, and retied its curtailed proportions around the waist. "It does feel a heap easier," she said, with a little shiver of satisfaction, as she lifted her round cheek, and the tail of her blue eyes with their brown lashes, over her shoulder. It was a tempting moment—but Jack felt that the whole race of gold hunters was on trial just then, and was adamant! Perhaps he was a gentle fellow at heart, too.

"I could loop up that dress also, if I had more pins," he remarked tentatively. Jack had sisters of his own.

The pins were forthcoming. In this operation—a kind of festooning—the girl's petticoat, a piece of common washed-out blue flannel, as pale as her eyes, but of the commonest material, became visible, but without fear or reproach to either.

"There, that looks more tidy," said Jack, critically surveying his work and a little of the small ankles revealed. The girl also examined it carefully by its reflection on the surface of the saucepan. "Looks a little like a chiny girl, don't it?"

Jack would have resented this, thinking she meant a Chinese, until he saw her pointing to a cheap crockery ornament, representing a Dutch shepherdess, on the shelf. There was some resemblance.

"You beat mammy out o' sight!" she exclaimed gleefully. "It will jest set her clear crazy when she sees me."

"Then you had better say you did it yourself," said Fleming.

"Why?" asked the girl, suddenly opening her eyes on him with relentless frankness.

"You said your father didn't like miners, and he mightn't like your lending your pan to me."

"I'm more afraid o' lyin' than o' dad," she said with an elevation of moral sentiment that was, however, slightly weakened by the addition, "Mammy'll say anything I'll tell her to say."

"Well, good-by," said Fleming, extending his hand.

"Ye didn't tell me what luck ye had with the pan," she said, delaying taking his hand.

Fleming shrugged his shoulders. "Oh, my usual luck,—nothing," he returned, with a smile.

"Ye seem to keer more for gettin' yer old ring back than for any luck," she continued. "I reckon you ain't much o' a miner."

"I'm afraid not."

"Ye didn't say wot yer name was, in case dad wants to know."

"I don't think he will want to; but it's John Fleming."

She took his hand. "You didn't tell me yours," he said, holding the little red fingers, "in case I wanted to know."

It pleased her to consider the rejoinder intensely witty. She showed all her little teeth, threw away his hand, and said:—

"G' long with ye, Mr. Fleming. It's Tinka"—

"Tinker?"

"Yes; short for Katinka,—Katinka Jallinger."

"Good-by, Miss Jallinger."

"Good-by. Dad's name is Henry Boone Jallinger, of Kentucky, ef ye was ever askin'."

"Thank you."

He turned away as she swiftly re-entered the house. As he walked away, he half expected to hear her voice uplifted again in the camp-meeting chant, but he was disappointed. When he reached the top of the hill he turned and looked back at the cabin.

She was apparently waiting for this, and waved him an adieu with the humble pan he had borrowed. It flashed a moment dazzlingly as it caught the declining sun, and then went out, even obliterating the little figure behind it.

PART II

Mr. Jack Fleming was indeed "not much of a miner." He and his partners—both as young, hopeful, and inefficient as himself—had for three months worked a claim in a mountain mining settlement which yielded them a certain amount of healthy exercise, good-humored grumbling, and exalted independence. To dig for three or four hours in the morning, smoke their pipes under a redwood-tree for an hour at noon, take up their labors again until sunset, when they "washed up" and gathered sufficient gold to pay for their daily wants, was, without their seeking it, or even knowing it, the realization of a charming socialistic ideal which better men than themselves had only dreamed of. Fleming fell back into this refined barbarism, giving little thought to his woodland experience, and no revelation of it to his partners. He had transacted their business at the mining town. His deviations en route were nothing to them, and small account to himself.

The third day after his return he was lying under a redwood when his partner approached him.

"You aren't uneasy in your mind about any unpaid bill—say a wash bill—that you're owing?"

"Why?"

"There's a big nigger woman in camp looking for you; she's got a folded account paper in her hand. It looks deucedly like a bill."

"There must be some mistake," suggested Fleming, sitting up.

"She says not, and she's got your name pat enough! Faulkner" (his other partner) "headed her straight up the gulch, away from camp, while I came down to warn you. So if you choose to skedaddle into the brush out there and lie low until we get her away, we'll fix it!"

"Nonsense! I'll see her."

His partner looked aghast at this temerity, but Fleming, jumping to his feet, at once set out to meet his mysterious visitor. This was no easy matter, as the ingenious Faulkner was laboriously leading his charge up the steep gulch road, with great politeness, but many audible misgivings as to whether this was not "Jack Fleming's day for going to Jamestown."

He was further lightening the journey by cheering accounts of the recent depredations of bears and panthers in that immediate locality. When overtaken by Fleming he affected a start of joyful surprise, to conceal the look of warning which Fleming did not heed,—having no eyes but for Faulkners companion. She was a very fat negro woman, panting with exertion and suppressed impatience. Fleming's heart was filled with compunction.

"Is you Marse Fleming?" she gasped.

"Yes," said Fleming gently. "What can I do for you?"

"Well! Ye kin pick dis yar insek, dis caterpillier," she said, pointing to Faulkner, "off my paf. Ye kin tell dis yar chipmunk dat when he comes to showin' me mule tracks for b'ar tracks, he's barkin' up de wrong tree! Dat when he tells me dat he sees panfers a-promenadin' round in de short grass or hidin' behime rocks in de open, he hain't talkin' to no nigger chile, but a growed woman! Ye kin tell him dat Mammy Curtis lived in de woods afo' he was born, and hez seen more b'ars and mountain lyuns dan he hez hairs in his mustarches."

The word "Mammy" brought a flash of recollection to Fleming.

"I am very sorry," he began; but to his surprise the negro woman burst into a good-tempered laugh.

"All right, honey! S'long's you is Marse Fleming and de man dat took dat 'ar pan offer Tinka de odder day, I ain't mindin' yo' frens' bedevilments. I've got somefin fo' you, yar, and a little box," and she handed him a folded paper.

Fleming felt himself reddening, he knew not why, at which Faulkner discreetly but ostentatiously withdrew, conveying to his other partner painful conviction that Fleming had borrowed a pan from a traveling tinker, whose negro wife was even now presenting a bill for the same, and demanding a settlement. Relieved by his departure, Fleming hurriedly tore open the folded paper. It was a letter written upon a leaf torn out of an old account book, whose ruled lines had undoubtedly given his partners the idea that it was a bill. Fleming hurriedly read the following, traced with a pencil in a schoolgirl's hand:—

Mr. J. Fleming.

Dear Sir,

After you went away that day I took that pan you brought back to mix a batch of bread and biscuits. The next morning at breakfast dad says: "What's gone o' them thar biscuits—my teeth is just broke with them—they're so gritty—they're abominable! What's this?" says he, and with that he chucks over to me two or three flakes of gold that was in them. You see what had happened, Mr. Fleming, was this! You had better luck than you was knowing of! It was this way! Some of the gold you washed had got slipped into the sides of the pan where it was broke, and the sticky dough must have brought it out, and I kneaded them up unbeknowing. Of course I had to tell a wicked lie, but "Be ye all things to all men," says the Book, and I thought you ought to know your good luck, and I send mammy with this and the gold in a little box. Of course, if dad was a hunter of Mammon and not of God's own beasts, he would have been mighty keen about finding where it came from, but he allows it was in the water in our near spring. So good-by. Do you care for your ring now as much as you did?

Yours very respectfully,
Katinka Jallinger.

As Mr. Fleming glanced up from the paper, mammy put a small cardboard box in his hand. For an instant he hesitated to open it, not knowing how far mammy was intrusted with the secret. To his great relief she said briskly: "Well, dar! now dat job's done gone and often my han's, I allow to quit and jest get off dis yer camp afo' ye kin shake a stick. So don't tell me nuffin I ain't gotter tell when I goes back."

Fleming understood. "You can tell her I thank her—and—I'll attend to it," he said vaguely; "that is—I"—

"Hold dar! that's just enuff, honey—no mo'! So long to ye and youse folks."

He watched her striding away toward the main road, and then opened the box.

It contained three flakes of placer or surface gold, weighing in all about a quarter of an ounce. They could easily have slipped into the interstices of the broken pan and not have been observed by him. If this was the result of the washing of a single pan—and he could now easily imagine that other flakes might have escaped—what—But he stopped, dazed and bewildered at the bare suggestion. He gazed upon the vanishing figure of "mammy." Could she—could Katinka—have the least suspicion of the possibilities of this discovery? Or had Providence put the keeping of this secret into the hands of those who least understood its importance? For an instant he thought of running after her with a word of caution; but on reflection he saw that this might awaken her suspicion and precipitate a discovery by another.

His only safety for the present was silence, until he could repeat his experiment. And that must be done quickly.

How should he get away without his partners' knowledge of his purpose? He was too loyal to them to wish to keep this good fortune to himself, but he was not yet sure of his good fortune. It might be only a little "pocket" which he had just emptied; it might be a larger one which another trial would exhaust.

He had put up no "notice;" he might find it already in possession of Katinka's father, or any chance prospector like himself. In either case he would be covered with ridicule by his partners and the camp, or more seriously rebuked for his carelessness and stupidity. No! he could not tell them the truth; nor could he lie. He would say he was called away for a day on private business.

Luckily for him, the active imagination of his partners was even now helping him. The theory of the "tinker" and the "pan" was indignantly rejected by his other partner. His blushes and embarrassment were suddenly remembered by Faulkner, and by the time he reached his cabin, they had settled that the negro woman had brought him a love letter! He was young and good looking; what was more natural than that he should have some distant love affair?

His embarrassed statement that he must leave early the next morning on business that he could not at *present* disclose was considered amply confirmatory, and received with maliciously significant acquiescence. "Only," said Faulkner, "at *your* age, sonny,"—he was nine months older than Fleming,— "I should have gone *to-night*." Surely Providence was favoring him!

He was off early the next morning. He was sorely tempted to go first to the cabin, but every moment was precious until he had tested the proof of his good fortune.

It was high noon before he reached the fringe of forest. A few paces farther and he found the spring and outcrop. To avert his partners' suspicions he had not brought his own implements, but had borrowed a pan, spade, and pick from a neighbor's claim before setting out. The spot was apparently in the same condition as when he left it, and with a beating heart he at once set to work, an easy task with his new implements. He nervously watched the water overflow the pan of dirt at its edges until, emptied of earth and gravel, the black sand alone covered the bottom. A slight premonition of disappointment followed; a rich indication would have shown itself before this! A few more workings, and the pan was quite empty except for a few pin-points of "color," almost exactly the quantity he found before. He washed another pan with the same result. Another taken from a different level of the outcrop yielded neither more nor less! There was no mistake: it was a failure! His discovery had been only a little "pocket," and the few flakes she had sent him were the first and last of that discovery.

He sat down with a sense of relief; he could face his partners again without disloyalty; he could see that pretty little figure once more without the compunction of having incurred her father's prejudices by locating a permanent claim so near his cabin. In fact, he could carry out his partners' fancy to the letter!

He quickly heaped his implements together and turned to leave the wood; but he was confronted by a figure that at first he scarcely recognized. Yet—it was Katinka! the young girl of the cabin, who had sent him the gold. She was dressed differently—perhaps in her ordinary every-day garments—a bright sprigged muslin, a chip hat with blue ribbons set upon a coil of luxurious brown hair. But what struck him most was that the girlish and diminutive character of the figure had vanished with her ill-fitting clothes; the girl that stood before him was of ordinary height, and of a prettiness and grace of figure that he felt would have attracted anywhere. Fleming felt himself suddenly embarrassed,—a feeling that was not lessened when he noticed that her pretty lip was compressed and her eyebrows a little straightened as she gazed at him.

"Ye made a bee line for the woods, I see," she said coldly. "I allowed ye might have been droppin' in to our house first."

"So I should," said Fleming quickly, "but I thought I ought to first make sure of the information you took the trouble to send me." He hesitated to speak of the ill luck he had just experienced; he could laugh at it himself—but would she?

"And ye got a new pan?" she said half poutingly.

Here seemed his opportunity. "Yes, but I'm afraid it hasn't the magic of yours. I haven't even got the color. I believe you bewitched your old pan."

Her face flushed a little and brightened, and her lip relaxed with a smile. "Go 'long with yer! Ye don't mean to say ye had no luck to-day?"

"None—but in seeing you."

Her eyes sparkled. "Ye see, I said all 'long ye weren't much o' a miner. Ye ain't got no faith. Ef ye had as much as a grain o' mustard seed, ye'd remove mountains; it's in the Book."

"Yes, and this mountain is on the bedrock, and my faith is not strong enough," he said laughingly. "And then, that would be having faith in Mammon, and you don't want me to have *that*."

She looked at him curiously. "I jest reckon ye don't care a picayune whether ye strike anything or not," she said half admiringly.

"To please you I'll try again, if you'll look on. Perhaps you'll bring me luck as you did before. You shall take the pan. I will fill it and you shall wash it out. You'll be my *mascot*."

She stiffened a little at this, and then said pertly, "Wot's that?"

"My good fairy."

She smiled again, this time with a new color in her pale face. "Maybe I am," she said, with sudden gravity.

He quickly filled the pan again with soil, brought it to the spring, and first washed out the greater bulk of loose soil. "Now come here and kneel down beside me," he said, "and take the pan and do as I show you."

She knelt down obediently. Suddenly she lifted her little hand with a gesture of warning. "Wait a minit—jest a minit—till the water runs clear again."

The pool had become slightly discolored from the first washing.

"That makes no difference," he said quickly.

"Ah! but wait, please!" She laid her brown hand upon his arm; a pleasant warmth seemed to follow her touch. Then she said joyously, "Look down there."

"Where?" he asked.

"There—don't ye see it?"

"See what?"

"You and me!"

He looked where she pointed. The pool had settled, resumed its mirror-like calm, and reflected distinctly, not only their two bending faces, but their two figures kneeling side by side. Two tall redwoods rose on either side of them, like the columns before an altar.

There was a moment of silence. The drone of a bumble-bee near by seemed to make the silence swim drowsily in their ears; far off they heard the faint beat of a woodpecker. The suggestion of their kneeling figures in this magic mirror was vague, unreasoning, yet for the moment none the less irresistible. His arm instinctively crept around her little waist as he whispered,—he scarce knew what he said,—"Perhaps here is the treasure I am seeking."

The girl laughed, released herself, and sprang up; the pan sank ingloriously to the bottom of the pool, where Fleming had to grope for it, assisted by Tinka, who rolled up her sleeve to her elbow. For a minute or two they washed gravely, but with no better success than attended his own individual efforts. The result in the bottom of the pan was the same. Fleming laughed.

"You see," he said gayly, "the Mammon of unrighteousness is not for me—at least, so near your father's tabernacle."

"That makes no difference now," said the girl quickly, "for dad is goin' to move, anyway, farther up the mountains. He says it's gettin' too crowded for him here—when the last settler took up a section three miles off."

"And are *you* going too?" asked the young man earnestly.

Tinka nodded her brown head. Fleming heaved a genuine sigh. "Well, I'll try my hand here a little longer. I'll put up a notice of claim; I don't suppose your father would object. You know he couldn't *legally*."

"I reckon ye might do it ef ye wanted—ef ye was *that* keen on gettin' gold!" said Tinka, looking away. There was something in the girl's tone which this budding lover resented. He had become sensitive.

"Oh, well," he said, "I see that it might make unpleasantness with your father. I only thought," he went on, with tenderer tentativeness, "that it would be pleasant to work here near you."

"Ye'd be only wastin' yer time," she said darkly.

Fleming rose gravely. "Perhaps you're right," he answered sadly and a little bitterly, "and I'll go at once."

He walked to the spring, and gathered up his tools. "Thank you again for your kindness, and good-by."

He held out his hand, which she took passively, and he moved away.

But he had not gone far before she called him. He turned to find her still standing where he had left her, her little hands clinched at her side, and her widely opened eyes staring at him. Suddenly she ran at him, and, catching the lapels of his coat in both hands, held him rigidly fast.

"No! no! ye sha'n't go—ye mustn't go!" she said, with hysterical intensity. "I want to tell ye something! Listen!—you—you—Mr. Fleming! I've been a wicked, wicked girl! I've told lies to dad—to mammy—to *you*! I've borne false witness—I'm worse than Sapphira—I've acted a big lie. Oh, Mr. Fleming, I've made you come back here for nothing! Ye didn't find no gold the other day. There wasn't any. It was all me! *I—I—salted that pan!*"

"Salted it!" echoed Fleming, in amazement.

"Yes, 'salted it,'" she faltered; "that's what dad says they call it—what those wicked sons of Mammon do to their claims to sell them. I—put gold in the pan myself; it wasn't there before."

"But why?" gasped Fleming.

She stopped. Then suddenly the fountains in the deep of her blue eyes were broken up; she burst into a sob, and buried her head in her hands, and her hands on his shoulder. "Because—because"—she sobbed against him—"*I wanted you* to come back!"

He folded her in his arms. He kissed her lovingly, forgivingly, gratefully, tearfully, smilingly—and paused; then he kissed her sympathetically, understandingly, apologetically, explanatorily, in lieu of other conversation. Then, becoming coherent, he asked,—

"But *where* did you get the gold?"

"Oh," she said between fitful and despairing sobs, "somewhere!—I don't know—out of the old Run—long ago—when I was little! I didn't never dare say anything to dad—he'd have been crazy mad at his own daughter diggin'—and I never cared nor thought a single bit about it until I saw you."

"And you have never been there since?"

"Never."

"Nor anybody else?"

"No."

Suddenly she threw back her head; her chip hat fell back from her face, rosy with a dawning inspiration! "Oh, say, Jack!—you don't think that—after all this time—there might"—She did not finish the sentence, but, grasping his hand, cried, "Come!"

She caught up the pan, he seized the shovel and pick, and they raced like boy and girl down the hill. When within a few hundred feet of the house she turned at right angles into the clearing, and saying, "Don't be skeered; dad's away," ran boldly on, still holding his hand, along the little valley. At its farther extremity they came to the "Run," a half-dried watercourse whose rocky sides were marked by the erosion of winter torrents. It was apparently as wild and secluded as the forest spring. "Nobody ever came here," said the girl hurriedly, "after dad sunk the well at the house."

One or two pools still remained in the Run from the last season's flow, water enough to wash out several pans of dirt.

Selecting a spot where the white quartz was visible, Fleming attacked the bank with the pick. After one or two blows it began to yield and crumble away at his feet. He washed out a panful perfunctorily, more intent on the girl than his work; she, eager, alert, and breathless, had changed places with him, and become the anxious prospector! But the result was the same. He threw away the pan with a laugh, to take her little hand! But she whispered, "Try again."

He attacked the bank once more with such energy that a great part of it caved and fell, filling the pan and even burying the shovel in the debris. He unearthed the latter while Tinka was struggling to get out the pan.

"The mean thing is stuck and won't move," she said pettishly. "I think it's broken now, too, just like ours."

Fleming came laughingly forward, and, putting one arm around the girl's waist, attempted to assist her with the other. The pan was immovable, and, indeed, seemed to be broken and bent. Suddenly he uttered an exclamation and began hurriedly to brush away the dirt and throw the soil out of the pan.

In another moment he had revealed a fragment of decomposed quartz, like discolored honeycombed cheese, half filling the pan. But on its side, where the pick had struck it glancingly, there was a yellow streak like a ray of sunshine! And as he strove to lift it he felt in that unmistakable omnipotency of weight that it was seamed and celled with gold.

The news of Mr. Fleming's engagement, two weeks later, to the daughter of the recluse religious hunter who had made a big strike at Lone Run, excited some skeptical discussion, even among the honest congratulations of his partners.

"That's a mighty queer story how Jack got that girl sweet on him just by borrowin' a prospectin' pan of her," said Faulkner, between the whiffs of his pipe under the trees. "You and me might have borrowed a hundred prospectin' pans and never got even a drink thrown in. Then to think of that old preachin' coon-hunter hevin' to give in and pass his strike over to his daughter's feller, jest because he had scruples about gold diggin' himself. He'd hev booted you and me outer his ranch first."

"Lord, ye ain't takin' no stock in that hogwash," responded the other. "Why, everybody knows old man Jallinger pretended to be sick o' miners and minin' camps, and couldn't bear to hev 'em near him, only jest because he himself was all the while secretly prospectin' the whole lode and didn't want no interlopers.

It was only when Fleming nippled in by gettin' hold o' the girl that Jallinger knew the secret was out, and that's the way he bought him off. Why, Jack wasn't no miner—never was—ye could see that. *He* never struck anything. The only treasure he found in the woods was Tinka Jallinger!"

A Belle of Canada City

Cissy was tying her hat under her round chin be-fore a small glass at her window. The window gave upon a background of serrated mountain and ol-ive-shadowed canyon, with a faint additional outline of a higher snow level—the only dreamy suggestion of the whole landscape. The foreground was a glar-ingly fresh and unpicturesque mining town, whose irregular attempts at regularity were set forth with all the cruel, uncompromising clearness of the Califor-nian atmosphere. There was the straight Main Street with its new brick block of "stores," ending abruptly against a tangled bluff; there was the ruthless clear-ing in the sedate pines where the hideous spire of the new church imitated the soaring of the solemn shafts it had displaced with almost irreligious mockery. Yet this foreground was Cissy's world—her life, her sole girlish experience. She did not, however, bother her pretty head with the view just then, but moved her cheek up and down before the glass, the better to examine by the merciless glare of the sunlight a few freckles that starred the hollows of her temples. Like others of her sex, she was a poor critic of what was her real beauty, and quarreled with that peculiar texture of her healthy skin which made her face as eloquent in her sun-kissed cheek as in her bright eyes and expression. Nevertheless, she was somewhat consoled by the ravishing effect of the bowknot she had just tied, and turned away not wholly dissatisfied. Indeed, as the acknowledged belle of Canada City and the daughter of its principal banker, small wonder that a certain frank vanity and childlike imperiousness were among her faults—and her attractions.

She bounded down the stairs and into the front parlor, for their house possessed the unheard-of luxury of a double drawing-room, albeit the second apartment contained a desk, and was occasionally used by Cissy's father in private business interviews with anxious seekers of "advances" who shunned the publicity of the bank. Here she instantly flew into the arms of her bosom friend, Miss Piney Tibbs, a girl only a shade or two less pretty than herself, who, always more or less ill at ease in these splendors, was awaiting her impatiently. For Miss Tibbs was merely the daughter of the hotel-keeper; and although Tibbs was a Southerner, and had owned "his own niggers" in the States, she was of inferior position and a protegee of Cissy's.

"Thank goodness you've come," exclaimed Miss Tibbs, "for I've bin sittin' here till I nigh took root. What kep' ye?"

"How does it look?" responded Cissy, as a relevant reply.

The "it" referred to Cissy's new hat, and to the young girl the coherence was perfectly plain. Miss Tibbs looked at "it" severely. It would not do for a protegee to be too complaisant.

"Hem! Must have cost a heap o' money."

"It did! Came from the best milliner in San Francisco."

"Of course," said Piney, with half assumed envy. "When your popper runs the bank and just wallows in gold!"

"Never mind, dear," replied Cissy cheerfully. "So'll *your* popper some day. I'm goin' to get mine to let *your* popper into something—Ditch stocks and such. Yes! True, O King! Popper'll do anything for me," she added a little loftily.

Loyal as Piney was to her friend, she was by no means convinced of this. She knew the difference between the two men, and had a vivid recollection of hearing her own father express his opinion of Cissy's respected parent as a "Gold Shark" and "Quartz Miner Crusher." It did not, however, affect her friendship for Cissy. She only said, "Let's come!" caught Cissy around the waist, pranced with her out into the veranda, and gasped, out of breath, "Where are we goin' first?"

"Down Main Street," said Cissy promptly.

"And let's stop at Markham's store. They've got some new things in from Sacramento," added Piney.

"Country styles," returned Cissy, with a supercilious air. "No! Besides, Markham's head clerk is gettin' too presumptuous. Just guess! He asked me, while I was buyin' something, if I enjoyed the dance last Monday!"

"But you danced with him," said the simple Piney, in astonishment.

"But not in his store among his customers," said Cissy sapiently. "No! we're going down Main Street past Secamps'. Those Secamp girls are sure to be at their windows, looking out. This hat will just turn 'em green—greener than ever."

"You're just horrid, Ciss!" said Piney, with admiration.

"And then," continued Cissy, "we'll just sail down past the new block to the parson's and make a call."

"Oh, I see," said Piney archly. "It'll be just about the time when the new engineer of the mill works has a clean shirt on, and is smoking his cigyar before the office."

Cissy tossed her hat disdainfully. "Much anybody cares whether he's there or not! I haven't forgotten how he showed us over the mill the other day in a pair of overalls, just like a workman."

"But they say he's awfully smart and well educated, and needn't work, and I'm sure it's very nice of him to dress just like the other men when he's with 'em," urged Piney.

"Bah! That was just to show that he didn't care what we thought of him, he's that conceited! And it wasn't respectful, considering one of the directors was there, all dressed up. Don't tell me! You can see it in his eye, looking you over without blinking and then turning away as if he'd got enough of you. He makes me tired."

Piney did not reply. The engineer had seemed to her to be a singularly attractive young man, yet she was equally impressed with Cissy's superior condition, which could find flaws in such perfection. Following her friend down the steps of the veranda, they passed into the staring graveled walk of the new garden, only recently recovered from the wild wood, its accurate diamond and heart shaped beds of vivid green set in white quartz borders giving it the appearance of elaborately iced confectionery. A few steps further brought them to the road and the wooden "sidewalk" to Main Street, which carried civic improvements to the hillside, and Mr. Trixit's very door. Turning down this thoroughfare, they stopped laughing, and otherwise assumed a conscious half artificial air; for it was the hour when Canada City lounged listlessly before its shops, its saloons, its offices and mills, or even held lazy meetings in the dust of the roadway, and the passage down the principal street of its two prettiest girls was an event to be viewed as if it were a civic procession. Hats flew off as they passed; place was freely given; impeding barrels and sacks were removed from the wooden pavement, and preoccupied indwellers hastily summoned to the front door to do homage to Cissy Trixit and Piney as they went by. Not but that Canada City, in the fierce and unregenerate days of its youth, had seen fairer and higher colored faces, more gayly bedizened, on its thoroughfares, but never anything so fresh and innocent. Men stood there all unconsciously, reverencing their absent mothers, sisters, and daughters, in their spontaneous homage to the pair, and seemed to feel the wholesome breath of their Eastern homes wafted from the freshly ironed skirts of these foolish virgins as they rustled by. I am afraid that neither Cissy nor Piney appreciated this feeling; few women did at that time; indeed, these young ladies assumed a slight air of hauteur.

"Really, they do stare so," said Cissy, with eyes dilating with pleasurable emotion; "we'll have to take the back street next time!"

Piney, proud in the glory reflected from Cissy, and in her own, answered, "We will—sure!"

There was only one interruption to this triumphal progress, and that was so slight as to be noticed by only one of the two girls. As they passed the new works at the mill, the new engineer, as Piney had foreseen, was leaning against the doorpost, smoking a pipe. He took his hat from his head and his pipe from his month as they approached, and greeted them with an easy "Good-afternoon," yet with a glance that was quietly observant and tolerantly critical.

"There!" said Cissy, when they had passed, "didn't I tell you? Did you ever see such conceit in your born days? I hope you did not look at him."

Piney, conscious of having done so, and of having blushed under his scrutiny, nevertheless stoutly asserted that she had merely looked at him "to see who it was." But Cissy was placated by passing the Secamps' cottage, from whose window the three strapping daughters of John Secamp, lately an emigrant from Missouri, were, as Cissy had surmised, lightening the household duties by gazing at the—to them—unwonted wonders of the street. Whether their complexions, still bearing traces of the alkali dust and inefficient nourishment of the plains, took a more yellow tone from the spectacle of Cissy's hat, I cannot say. Cissy thought they did; perhaps Piney was nearer the truth when she suggested that they were only "looking" to enable them to make a home-made copy of the hat next week.

Their progress forward and through the outskirts of the town was of the same triumphal character. Teamsters withheld their oaths and their uplifted whips as the two girls passed by; weary miners, toiling in ditches, looked up with a pleasure that was half reminiscent of their past; younger skylarkers stopped in their horse-play with half smiling, half apologetic faces; more ambitious riders on the highway urged their horses to greater speed under the girls' inspiring eyes, and "Vaquero Billy," charging them, full tilt, brought up his mustang on its haunches and rigid forelegs, with a sweeping bow of his sombrero, within a foot of their artfully simulated terror! In this way they at last reached the clearing in the forest, the church with its ostentatious spire, and the Reverend Mr. Windibrook's dwelling, otherwise humorously known as "The Pastorage," where Cissy intended to call.

The Reverend Mr. Windibrook had been selected by his ecclesiastical superiors to minister to the spiritual wants of Canada City as being what was called a "hearty" man. Certainly, if considerable lung capacity, absence of reserve, and power of handshaking and back slapping were necessary to the redemption of Canada City, Mr. Windibrook's ministration would have been successful. But, singularly enough, the rude miner was apt to resent this familiarity, and it is recorded that Isaac Wood, otherwise known as "Grizzly Woods," once responded to a cheerful back slap from the reverend gentleman by an ostentatiously friendly hug which nearly dislocated the parson's ribs. Perhaps Mr. Windibrook was more popular on account of his admiring enthusiasm of the prosperous money-getting members of his flock and a singular sympathy with their methods, and Mr. Trixit's daring speculations were an especially delightful theme to him.

"Ah, Miss Trixit," he said, as Cissy entered the little parlor, "and how is your dear father? Still startling the money market with his fearless speculations? This, brother Jones," turning to a visitor, "is the daughter of our Napoleon of finance, Montagu Trixit. Only last week, in that deal in 'the Comstock,' he cleared fifty thousand dollars! Yes, sir," repeating it with unction, "fifty—thousand—dollars!—in about two hours, and with a single stroke of the pen! I believe I am not overstating, Miss Trixit?" he added, appealing to Cissy with a portentous politeness that was as badly fitting as his previous "heartiness."

Cissy colored slightly. "I don't know," she said simply. She was perfectly truthful. She knew nothing of her father's business, except the vague reputation of his success.

Her modesty, however, produced a singular hilarity in Mr. Windibrook, and a playful push. "*You* don't know? Ha, but I do. Yes, sir,"—to the visitor,—"I have reason to remember it. I called upon him the next day. I used, sir, the freedom of an old friend. 'Trixit,' I said, clapping my hand on his shoulder, 'the Lord has been good to you. I congratulate you.'

"'H'm!' he said, without looking up. 'What do you reckon those congratulations are worth?'

"Many a man, sir, who didn't know his style, would have been staggered. But I knew my man. I looked him straight in the eye. 'A new organ,' I said, 'and as good a one as Sacramento can turn out.'

"He took up a piece of paper, scrawled a few lines on it to his cashier, and said, 'Will that do?'" Mr. Windibrook's voice sank to a thrilling whisper. "It was an order for one thousand dollars! Fact, sir. *That* is the father of this young lady."

"Ye had better luck than Bishop Briggs had with old Johnson, the Excelsior Bank president," said the visitor, encouraged by Windibrook's "heartiness" into a humorous retrospect. "Briggs goes to him for a subscription for a new fence round the buryin'-ground—the old one havin' rotted away. 'Ye don't want no fence,' sez Johnson, short like. 'No fence round a buryin'-ground?' sez Briggs, starin'. 'No! Them as is *in* the buryin'-ground can't get *out*, and them as *isn't* don't want to get *in*, nohow! So you kin just travel—I ain't givin' money away on uselessnesses!' Ha! ha!"

A chill silence followed, which checked even Piney's giggle. Mr. Windibrook evidently had no "heartiness" for non-subscribing humor. "There are those who can jest with sacred subjects," he said ponderously, "but I have always found Mr. Trixit, though blunt, eminently practical. Your father is still away," he added, shifting the conversation to Cissy, "hovering wherever he can extract the honey to store up for the provision of age. An industrious worker."

"He's still away," said Cissy, feeling herself on safe ground, though she was not aware of her father's entomological habits. "In San Francisco, I think."

She was glad to get away from Mr. Windibrook's "heartiness" and console herself with Mrs. Windibrook's constitutional depression, which was partly the result of nervous dyspepsia and her husband's boisterous cordiality. "I suppose, dear, you are dreadfully anxious about your father when he is away from home?" she said to Cissy, with a sympathetic sigh.

Cissy, conscious of never having felt a moment's anxiety, and accustomed to his absences, replied naively, "Why?"

"Oh," responded Mrs. Windibrook, "on account of his great business responsibilities, you know; so much depends upon him."

Again Cissy did not comprehend; she could not understand why this masterful man, her father, who was equal to her own and, it seemed, everybody's needs, had any responsibility, or was not as infallible and constant as the sunshine or the air she breathed. Without being his confidante, or even his associate, she had since her mother's death no other experience; youthfully alive to the importance of their wealth, it seemed to her, however, only a natural result of being *his* daughter. She smiled vaguely and a little impatiently. They might have talked to her about *herself*; it was a little tiresome to always have to answer questions about her "popper." Nevertheless, she availed herself of Mrs. Windibrook's invitation to go into the garden and see the new summerhouse that had been put up among the pines, and gradually diverted her hostess's conversation into gossip of the town. If it was somewhat lugubrious and hesitating, it was, however, a relief to Cissy, and bearing chiefly upon the vicissitudes of others, gave her the comforting glow of comparison.

Touching the complexion of the Secamp girls, Mrs. Windibrook attributed it to their great privations in the alkali desert. "One day," continued Mrs. Windibrook, "when their father was ill with fever and ague, they drove the cattle twenty miles to water through that dreadful poisonous dust, and when they got there their lips were cracked and bleeding and their eyelids like burning knives, and Mamie Secamp's hair, which used to be a beautiful brown like your own, my dear, was bleached into a rusty yellow."

"And they *will* wear colors that don't suit them," said Cissy impatiently.

"Never mind, dear," said Mrs. Windibrook ambig-
uously; "I suppose they will have their reward."

Nor was the young engineer discussed in a lighter
vein. "It pains me dreadfully to see that young man
working with the common laborers and giving himself no rest, just because he says he wants to know
exactly 'how the thing is done' and why the old works
failed," she remarked sadly. "When Mr. Windibrook
knew he was the son of Judge Masterton and had rich
relations, he wished, of course, to be civil, but somehow young Masterton and he didn't 'hit off.' Indeed,
Mr. Windibrook was told that he had declared that
the prosperity of Canada City was only a mushroom
growth, and it seems too shocking to repeat, dear, but
they say he said that the new church—*our* church—
was simply using the Almighty as a big bluff to the
other towns. Of course, Mr. Windibrook couldn't see
him after that. Why, he even said your father ought to
send you to school somewhere, and not let you grow
up in this half civilized place."

Strangely enough, Cissy did not hail this corroboration of her dislike to young Masterton with the
liveliness one might have expected. Perhaps it was
because Piney Tibbs was no longer present, having
left Cissy at the parsonage and returned home. Still
she enjoyed her visit after a fashion, romped with the
younger Windibrooks and climbed a tree in the se-
curity of her sylvan seclusion and the promptings of
her still healthy, girlish blood, and only came back
to cake and tea and her new hat, which she had

prudently hung up in the summer-house, as the afternoon was waning. When they returned to the house, they found that Mr. Windibrook had gone out with his visitor, and Cissy was spared the advertisement of a boisterous escort home, which he generally insisted upon. She gayly took leave of the infant Windibrook and his mother, sallied out into the empty road, and once more became conscious of her new hat.

The shadows were already lengthening, and a cool breeze stirred the deep aisles of the pines on either side of the highway. One or two people passed her hurriedly, talking and gesticulating, evidently so preoccupied that they did not notice her. Again, a rapid horseman rode by without glancing round, overtook the pedestrians, exchanged a few hurried words with them, and then spurred swiftly away as one of them shouted after him, "There's another dispatch confirming it." A group of men talking by the roadside failed to look up as she passed. Cissy pouted slightly at this want of taste, which made some late election news or the report of a horse race more enthralling than her new hat and its owner. Even the toilers in the ditches had left their work, and were congregated around a man who was reading aloud from a widely margined "extra" of the "Canada City Press." It seemed provoking, as she knew her cheeks were glowing from her romp, and was conscious that she was looking her best. However, the Secamps' cottage was just before her, and the girls were sure to be on the lookout! She shook out her skirts and straightened her pretty little figure as she approached the house. But to her surprise, her coming had evidently been anticipated by them, and they were actually—and unexpectedly—awaiting her behind the low whitewashed garden palings! As she neared them they burst into a shrill, discordant laugh, so full of irony, gratified malice, and mean exaltation that Cissy was for a moment startled. But only for a moment; she had her father's reckless audacity, and bore them down with a display of such pink cheeks and flashing eyes that their laughter was checked, and they remained open-mouthed as she swept by them.

Perhaps this incident prevented her from noticing another but more passive one. A group of men standing before the new mill—the same men who had so solicitously challenged her attention with their bows a couple of hours ago—turned as she approached and suddenly dispersed. It was not until this was repeated by another group that its oddity forced itself upon her still angry consciousness. Then the street seemed to be full of those excited preoccupied groups who melted away as she advanced. Only one man met her curious eyes,—the engineer,—yet she missed the usual critical smile with which he was wont to greet her, and he gave her a bow of such profound respect and gravity that for the first time she felt really uneasy. Was there something wrong with her hat? That dreadful, fateful hat! Was it too conspicuous? Did he think it was vulgar? She was eager to cross the street on the next block where there were large plate-glass windows which she and Piney—if Piney were only with her now!—had often used as mirrors.

But there was a great crowd on the next block, congregated around the bank,—her father's bank! A vague terror, she knew not what, now began to creep over her. She would have turned into a side street, but mingled with her fear was a resolution not to show it,—not to even *think* of it,—to combat it as she had combated the horrid laugh of the Secamp girls, and she kept her way with a beating heart but erect head, without looking across the street.

There was another crowd before the newspaper office—also on the other side—and a bulletin board, but she would not try to read it. Only one idea was in her mind,—to reach home before any one should speak to her; for the last intelligible sound that had reached her was the laugh of the Secamp girls, and this was still ringing in her ears, seeming to voice the hidden strangeness of all she saw, and stirring her, as that had, with childish indignation. She kept on with unmoved face, however, and at last turned into the planked side-terrace,—a part of her father's munificence,—and reached the symmetrical garden-beds and graveled walk. She ran up the steps of the veranda and entered the drawing-room through the open French window. Glancing around the familiar room, at her father's closed desk, at the open piano with the piece of music she had been practicing that morning, the whole walk seemed only a foolish dream that had frightened her. She was Cissy Trixit, the daughter of the richest man in the town! This was her father's house, the wonder of Canada City!

A ring at the front doorbell startled her; without waiting for the servant to answer it, she stepped out on the veranda, and saw a boy whom she recognized as a waiter at the hotel kept by Piney's father. He was holding a note in his hand, and staring intently at the house and garden. Seeing Cissy, he transferred his stare to her. Snatching the note from him, she tore it open, and read in Piney's well-known scrawl, "Dad won't let me come to you now, dear, but I'll try to slip out late to-night." Why should she want to come? She had said nothing about coming *now*—and why should her father prevent her? Cissy crushed the note between her fingers, and faced the boy.

"What are you staring at—idiot?"

The boy grinned hysterically, a little frightened at Cissy's straightened brows and snapping eyes.

"Get away! there's no answer."

The boy ran off, and Cissy returned to the drawing-room. Then it occurred to her that the servant had not answered the bell. She rang again furiously. There was no response. She called down the basement staircase, and heard only the echo of her voice in the depths. How still the house was! Were they *all* out,—Susan, Norah, the cook, the Chinaman, and the gardener? She ran down into the kitchen; the back door was open, the fires were burning, dishes were upon the table, but the kitchen was empty. Upon the floor lay a damp copy of the "extra." She picked it up quickly. Several black headlines stared her in the face. "Enormous Defalcation!" "Montagu Trixit Absconded!" "50,000 Dollars Missing!" "Run on the Bank!"

She threw the paper through the open door as she would have hurled back the accusation from living lips. Then, in a revulsion of feeling lest any one should find her there, she ran upstairs and locked herself in her own room.

So that was what it all meant! All!—from the laugh of the Secamp girls to the turning away of the towns-people as she went by. Her father was a thief who had stolen money from the bank and run away leaving her alone to bear it! No! It was all a lie—a wicked, jealous lie! A foolish lie, for how could he steal money from *his own* bank? Cissy knew very little of her father— perhaps that was why she believed in him; she knew still less of business, but she knew that *he* did. She had often heard them say it—perhaps the very ones who now called him names. He! who had made Canada City what it was! *He*, who, Windibrook said, only to-day, had, like Moses, touched the rocks of the Canada with his magic wand of Finance, and streams of public credit and prosperity had gushed from it! She would never speak to them again! She would shut herself up here, dismiss all the servants but the Chinaman, and wait until her father returned.

There was a knock, and the entreating voice of Norah, the cook, outside the door. Cissy unlocked it and flung it open indignantly.

"Ah! It's yourself, miss—and I never knew ye kem back till I met that gossoon of a hotel waiter in the street," said the panting servant. "Sure it was only an hour ago while I was at me woorrck in the kitchen, and Jim rushes in and sez: 'For the love of God, if iver ye want to see a blessed cint of the money ye put in the masther's bank, off wid ye now and draw it out—for there's a run on the bank!'"

"It was an infamous lie," said Cissy fiercely.

"Sure, miss, how was oi to know? And if the masther *has* gone away, it's ownly takin' me money from the other divils down there that's drawin' it out and dividin' it betwixt and between them."

Cissy had a very vague idea of what a "run on the bank" meant, but Norah's logic seemed to satisfy her feminine reason. She softened a little.

"Mr. Windibrook is in the parlor, miss, and a jintleman on the veranda," continued Norah, encouraged.

Cissy started. "I'll come down," she said briefly.

Mr. Windibrook was waiting beside the piano, with his soft hat in one hand and a large white handkerchief in the other. He had confidently expected to find Cissy in tears, and was ready with boisterous condolement, but was a little taken aback as the young girl entered with a pale face, straightened brows, and eyes that shone with audacious rebellion. However, it was too late to change his attitude. "Ah, my young friend," he said a little awkwardly, "we must not give way to our emotions, but try to recognize in our trials the benefits of a great lesson. But," he added hurriedly, seeing her stand still silent but erect before him, "I see that you do!" He paused, coughed slightly, cast a glance at the veranda,—where Cissy now for the first time observed a man standing in an obviously assumed attitude of negligent abstraction,—moved towards the back room, and in a lower voice said, "A word with you in private."

Without replying, Cissy followed him.

"If," said Mr. Windibrook, with a sickly smile, "you are questioned regarding your father's affairs, you may remember his peculiar and utterly unsolicited gift of a certain sum towards a new organ, to which I alluded to-day. You can say that he always expressed great liberality towards the church, and it was no surprise to you."

Cissy only stared at him with dangerous eyes.

"Mrs. Windibrook," continued the reverend gentleman in his highest, heartiest voice, albeit a little hurried, "wished me to say to you that until you heard from—your friends—she wanted you to come and stay with her. *Do* come! *Do!*"

Cissy, with her bright eyes fixed upon her visitor, said, "I shall stay here."

"But," said Mr. Windibrook impatiently, "you cannot. That man you see on the veranda is the sheriff's officer. The house and all that it contains are in the hands of the law."

Cissy's face whitened in proportion as her eyes grew darker, but she said stoutly, "I shall stay here till my popper tells me to go."

"Till your popper tells you to go!" repeated Mr. Windibrook harshly, dropping his heartiness and his handkerchief in a burst of unguarded temper. "Your papa is a thief escaping from justice, you foolish girl; a disgraced felon, who dare not show his face again in Canada City; and you are lucky, yes! lucky, miss, if you do not share his disgrace!"

"And you're a wicked, wicked liar!" said Cissy, clinching her little fists at her side and edging towards him with a sidelong bantam-like movement as she advanced her freckled cheek close to his with an effrontery so like her absconding father that he recoiled before it. "And a mean, double-faced hypocrite, too! Didn't you always praise him? Didn't you call him a Napoleon, and a—Moses? Didn't you say he was the making of Canada City? Didn't you get him to raise your salary, and start a subscription for your new house? Oh, you—you—stinking beast!"

Here the stranger on the veranda, still gazing abstractedly at the landscape, gave a low and apparently unconscious murmur, as if enraptured with the view. Mr. Windibrook, recalled to an attempt at dignity, took up his hat and handkerchief. "When you have remembered yourself and your position, Miss Trixit," he said loftily, "the offer I have made you"—

"I despise it! I'd sooner stay in the woods with the grizzlies and rattlesnakes?" said Cissy pantingly. "Go and leave me alone! Do you hear?" She stamped her little foot. "Are you listening? Go!"

Mr. Windibrook promptly retreated through the door and down the steps into the garden, at which the stranger on the veranda reluctantly tore himself away from the landscape and slowly entered the parlor through the open French window. Here, however, he became equally absorbed and abstracted in the condition of his beard, carefully stroking his shaven cheek and lips and pulling his goatee.

After a pause he turned to the angry Cissy, standing by the piano, radiant with glowing cheeks and flashing eyes, and said slowly, "I reckon you gave the parson as good as he sent. It kinder settles a man to hear the frozen truth about himself sometimes, and you've helped old Shadbelly considerably on the way towards salvation. But he was right about one thing, Miss Trixit. The house IS in the hands of the law. I'm representing it as deputy sheriff. Mebbe you might remember me—Jake Poole—when your father was addressing the last Citizen's meeting, sittin' next to him on the platform—*I'm* in possession. It isn't a job I'm hankerin' much arter; I'd a lief rather hunt hoss thieves or track down road agents than this kind o' fancy, underhand work. So you'll excuse me, miss, if I ain't got the style." He paused, rubbed his chin thoughtfully, and then said slowly and with great deliberation: "Ef there's any little thing here, miss,—any keepsakes or such trifles ez you keer for in partickler, things you wouldn't like strangers to have,—you just make a little pile of 'em and drop 'em down somewhere outside the back door. There ain't no inventory taken

nor sealin' up of anythin' done just yet, though I have
to see there ain't anythin' disturbed. But I kalkilate
to walk out on that veranda for a spell and look at the
landscape." He paused again, and said, with a sigh of
satisfaction, "It's a mighty pooty view out thar; it just
takes me every time."

As he turned and walked out through the French
window, Cissy did not for a moment comprehend
him; then, strangely enough, his act of rude courtesy
for the first time awakened her to the full sense of the
situation. This house, her father's house, was no longer hers! If her father should *never* return, she wanted nothing from it, *nothing*! She gripped her beating
heart with the little hand she had clinched so valiant-
ly a moment ago. Suddenly her hand dropped. Some
one had glided noiselessly into the back room; a figure
in a blue blouse; a Chinaman, their house servant, Ah
Fe. He cast a furtive glance at the stranger on the veranda, and then beckoned to her stealthily. She came
towards him wonderingly, when he suddenly whipped
a note from his sleeve, and with a dexterous movement
slipped it into her fingers. She tore it open. A single
glance showed her a small key inclosed in a line of
her father's handwriting. Drawing quickly back into
the corner, she read as follows: "If this reaches you
in time, take from the second drawer of my desk an
envelope marked 'Private Contracts' and give it to the
bearer." There was neither signature nor address.

Putting her finger to her lips, she cast a quick
glance at the absorbed figure on the veranda and

stepped before the desk. She fitted the key to the drawer and opened it rapidly but noiselessly. There lay the envelope, and among other ticketed papers a small roll of greenbacks—such as her father often kept there. It was *his* money; she did not scruple to take it with the envelope. Handing the latter to the Chinaman, who made it instantly disappear up his sleeve like a conjurer's act, she signed him to follow her into the hall.

"Who gave you that note, Ah Fe?" she whispered breathlessly.

"Chinaman."

"Who gave it to him?"

"Chinaman."

"And to *him*?"

"Nollee Chinaman."

"Another Chinaman?"

"Yes—heap Chinaman—allee same as gang."

"You mean it passed from one Chinaman's hand to another?"

"Allee same."

"Why didn't the first Chinaman who got it bring it here?"

"S'pose Mellikan man want to catchee lettel. He spotty Chinaman. He follee Chinaman. Chinaman passee lettel nex' Chinaman. He no get. Mellikan man no habe got. Sabe?"

"Then this package will go back the same way?"

"Allee same."

"And who will *you* give it to now?"

"Allee same man blingee me lettel. Hop Li—who makee washee."

An idea here struck Cissy which made her heart jump and her cheeks flame. Ah Fe gazed at her with an infantile smile of admiration.

"How far did that letter come?" she asked, with eager questioning eyes.

"Lettee me see him," said Ah Fe.

Cissy handed him the missive; he examined closely some half-a-dozen Chinese characters that were scrawled along the length of the outer fold, and which she had innocently supposed were a part of the markings of the rice paper on which the note was written.

"Heap Chinaman velly much walkee—longee way! S'pose you look." He pointed through the open front door to the prospect beyond. It was a familiar one to Cissy,—the long Canada, the crest on crest of serried pines, and beyond the dim snow-line. Ah Fe's brown finger seemed to linger there.

"In the snow," she whispered, her cheek whitening like that dim line, but her eyes sparkling like the sunshine over it.

"Allee same, John," said Ah Fe plaintively.

"Ah Fe," whispered Cissy, "take *me* with you to Hop Li."

"No good," said Ah Fe stolidly. "Hop Li, he givee this"—he indicated the envelope in his sleeve—"to next Chinaman. *He* no go. S'pose you go with me, Hop Li—you no makee nothing—allee same, makee foolee!"

"I know; but you just take me there. *Do!*"

The young girl was irresistible. Ah Fe's face relaxed. "Allee litee!" he said, with a resigned smile.

"You wait here a moment," said Cissy, brightening. She flew up the staircase. In a few minutes she was back again. She had exchanged her smart rose-sprigged chintz for a pathetic little blue-checked frock of her school-days; the fateful hat had given way to a brown straw "flat," bent like a frame around her charming face. All the girlishness, and indeed a certain honest boyishness of her nature, seemed to have come out in her glowing, freckled cheek, brilliant, audacious eyes, and the quick stride which brought her to Ah Fe's side.

"Now let's go," she said, "out the back way and down the side streets." She paused, cast a glance through the drawing-room at the contemplative figure of the sheriff's deputy on the veranda, and then passed out of the house forever.

The excitement over the failure of Montagu Trixit's bank did not burn itself out until midnight. By that time, however, it was pretty well known that the amount of the defalcations had been exaggerated; that it had been preceded by the suspension of the "Excelsior Bank" of San Francisco, of which Trixit was also a managing director, occasioned by the discovery of the withdrawal of securities for use in the branch bank at Canada City; that he had fled the State eastward across the Sierras; yet that, owing to the vigilance of the police on the frontier, he had failed to escape and was in hiding. But there were adverse reports of a more sinister nature. It was said that others were implicated; that they dared not bring him to justice; it was pointed out that there was more concern among many who were not openly connected with the bank than among its unfortunate depositors. Besides the inevitable downfall of those who had invested their fortunes in it, there was distrust or suspicion everywhere. Even Trixit's enemies were forced to admit the saying that "Canada City was the bank, and the bank was Trixit."

Perhaps this had something to do with an excited meeting of the directors of the New Mill, to whose discussions Dick Masterton, the engineer, had been hurriedly summoned. When the president told him that he had been selected to undertake the difficult and delicate mission of discovering the whereabouts of Montagu Trixit, and, if possible, procuring an interview with him, he was amazed. What had the New Mill, which had always kept itself aloof from the bank and its methods, to do with the disgraced manager? He was still more astonished when the president added bluntly:—

"Trixit holds securities of ours for money advanced to the mill by himself privately. They do not appear on the books, but if he chooses to declare them as assets of the bank, it's a bad thing for us. If he is bold enough to keep them, he may be willing to make some arrangement with us to carry them on. If he has got away or committed suicide, as some say, it's for you to find the whereabouts of the securities and get them. He is said to have been last seen near the Summit. You understand our position?"

Masterton did, with suppressed disgust. But he was young, and there was the thrill of adventure in this. "I will go," he said quietly.

"We thought you would. You must take the up stage to-night. Come again and get your final instructions. By the way, you might get some information at Trixit's house. You—er—er—are acquainted with his daughter, I think?"

"Which makes it quite impossible for me to seek her for such a purpose," said Masterton coldly.

A few hours later he was on the coach. As they cleared the outskirts of the town, they passed two Chinamen plodding sturdily along in the dust of the highway.

Mr. Masterton started from a slight doze in the heavy, lumbering "mountain wagon" which had taken the place of the smart Concord coach that he had left at the last station. The scenery, too, had changed; the four horses threaded their way through rocky defiles of stunted larches and hardy "brush," with here and there open patches of shrunken snow. Yet at the edge of declivities he could still see through the rolled-up leather curtains the valley below bathed in autumn,

the glistening rivers half spent with the long summer drought, and the green slopes rolling upward into
crest after crest of ascending pines. At times a drifting haze, always imperceptible from below, veiled the
view; a chill wind blew through the vehicle, and made
the steel sledge-runners that hung beneath the wagon,
ready to be shipped under the useless wheels, an omi-
nous provision. A few rude "stations," half blacksmith
shops, half grocery, marked the deserted but wellworn
road; along, narrow "packer's" wagon, or a tortuous file
of Chinamen carrying mysterious bundles depending
from bamboo poles, was their rare and only company.
The rough sheepskin jackets which these men wore
over their characteristic blue blouses and their heavy
leggings were a new revelation to Masterton, accustomed to the thinly clad coolie of the mines. They
seemed a distinct race.

"I never knew those chaps get so high up, but they
seem to understand the cold," he remarked.

The driver looked up, and ejaculated his disgust
and his tobacco juice at the same moment.

"I reckon they're everywhar in Californy whar you
want 'em and whar you don't; you take my word for it,
afore long Californy will hev to reckon that she gin-
erally *don't* want 'em, ef a white man has to live here.
With a race tied up together in a language ye can't
understand, ways that no feller knows,—from their
prayin' to devils, swappin' their wives, and havin' their
bones sent back to Chiny,—wot are ye goin' to do, and
where are ye? Wot are ye goin' to make outer men that

look so much alike ye can't tell 'em apart; that think alike and act alike, and never in ways that ye kin catch on to! Fellers knotted together in some underhand secret way o' communicatin' with each other, so that ef ye kick a Chinaman up here on the Summit, another Chinaman will squeal in the valley! And the way they do it just gets me! Look yer! I'll tell ye somethin' that happened, that's gospel truth! Some of the boys that reckoned to hev some fun with the Chinee gang over at Cedar Camp started out one afternoon to raid 'em. They groped along through the woods whar nobody could see 'em, kalkilatin' to come down with a rush on the camp, over two miles away. And nobody *did* see 'em, only *one* Chinaman wot they met a mile from the camp, burnin' punk to his joss or devil, and he scooted away just in the contrary direction. Well, sir, when they waltzed into that camp, darn my skin! ef there was a Chinaman there, or as much as a grain of rice to grab! Somebody had warned 'em! Well! this sort o' got the boys, and they set about discoverin' how it was done. One of 'em noticed that there was some of them bits of tissue paper slips that they toss around at funerals lyin' along the road near the camp, and another remembered that the Chinaman they met on the hill tossed a lot of that paper in the air afore he scooted. Well, sir, the wind carried just enough of that paper straight down the hill into that camp ten minutes afore *they* could get there, to give them Chinamen warnin'—whatever it was! Fact! Why, I've seen 'em stringin' along the road just like them fellers we passed just now, and then stop all of a suddent like hounds off the scent, jabber among themselves, and start off in a different direction"—

"Just what they're doing now! By thunder!" interrupted another passenger, who was looking through the rolled-up curtain at his side.

All the passengers turned by one accord and looked out. The file of Chinamen under observation had indeed turned, and was even then moving rapidly away at right angles from the road.

"Got some signal, you bet!" said the driver; "some yeller paper or piece o' joss stick in the road. What?"

The remark was addressed to the passenger who had just placed his finger on his lip, and indicated a stolid-looking Chinaman, overlooked before, who was sitting in the back or "steerage" seat.

"Oh, he be darned!" said the driver impatiently. "*He* is no account; he's only the laundryman from Rocky Canyon. I'm talkin' of the coolie gang."

But here the conversation flagged, and the air growing keener, the flaps of the leather side curtains were battened down. Masterton gave himself up to conflicting reflections. The information that he had gathered was meagre and unsatisfactory, and he could only trust to luck and circumstance to fulfill his mission. The first glow of adventure having passed, he was uneasily conscious that the mission was not to his taste. The pretty, flushed but defiant face of Cissy that afternoon haunted him; he had not known the immediate cause of it, but made no doubt that she had already heard the news of her father's disgrace when he met her. He regretted now that he hadn't spoken to her, if only a few formal words of sympathy. He had always been half tenderly amused at her frank conceit and her "airs,"—the innocent, undisguised pride of the country belle, so different from the hard aplomb of the city girl! And now the foolish little moth, dancing in the sunshine of prosperity, had felt the chill of winter in its pretty wings. The contempt he had for the father had hitherto shown itself in tolerant pity for the daughter, so proud of her father's position and what it brought her. In the revelation that his own directors had availed themselves of that father's methods, and the ignoble character of his present mission, he felt a stirring of self-reproach. What would become of her? Of course, frivolous as she was, she would not feel the keenness of this misfortune like another, nor yet rise superior to it. She would succumb for the present, to revive another season in a dimmer glory elsewhere. His critical, cynical observation of her had determined that any filial affection she might have would be merged and lost in the greater deprivation of her position.

A sudden darkening of the landscape below, and a singular opaque whitening of the air around them, aroused him from his thoughts. The driver drew up the collar of his overcoat and laid his whip smartly over the backs of his cattle. The air grew gradually darker, until suddenly it seemed to disintegrate into invisible gritty particles that swept through the wagon.

Presently these particles became heavier, more percep-
tible, and polished like small shot, and a keen wind
drove them stingingly into the faces of the passengers,
or insidiously into their pockets, collars, or the folds
of their clothes. The snow forced itself through the
smallest crevice.

"We'll get over this when once we've passed the
bend; the road seems to dip beyond," said Masterton
cheerfully from his seat beside the driver.

The driver gave him a single scornful look, and
turned to the passenger who occupied the seat on the
other side of him. "I don't like the look o' things down
there, but ef we are stuck, we'll have to strike out for
the next station."

"But," said Masterton, as the wind volleyed the
sharp snow pellets in their faces and the leaders were
scarcely distinguishable through the smoke-like dis-
charges, "it can't be worse than here."

The driver did not speak, but the other passenger
craned over his back, and said explanatorily:—

"I reckon ye don't know these storms; this kind o'
dry snow don't stick and don't clog. Look!"

Indeed, between the volleys, Masterton could see
that the road was perfectly bare and wind-swept, and
except slight drifts and banks beside outlying bushes
and shrubs,—which even then were again blown away
before his eyes,—the level landscape was unclothed
and unchanged. Where these mysterious snow pellets
went to puzzled and confused him; they seemed to
vanish, as they had appeared, into the air about them.

"I'd make a straight rush for the next station," said the other passenger confidently to the driver. "If we're stuck, we're that much on the way; if we turn back now, we'll have to take the grade anyway when the storm's over, and neither you nor I know when *that*'ll be. It may be only a squall just now, but it's gettin' rather late in the season. Just pitch in and drive all ye know."

The driver laid his lash on the horses, and for a few moments the heavy vehicle dashed forward in violent conflict with the storm. At times the elastic hickory framework of its domed leather roof swayed and bent like the ribs of an umbrella; at times it seemed as if it would be lifted bodily off; at times the whole interior of the vehicle was filled with a thin smoke by drifts through every cranny. But presently, to Masterton's great relief, the interminable level seemed to end, and between the whitened blasts he could see that the road was descending. Again the horses were urged forward, and at last he could feel that the vehicle began to add the momentum of its descent to its conflict with the storm. The blasts grew less violent, or became only the natural resistance of the air to their dominant rush. With the cessation of the snow volleys and the clearing of the atmosphere, the road became more strongly defined as it plunged downward to a terrace on the mountain flank, several hundred feet below. Presently they came again upon a thicker growth of bushes, and here and there a solitary fir. The wind died away; the cold seemed to be less bitter. Masterton, in his relief, glanced smilingly at his companions on the box, but the driver's mouth was compressed as he urged his team forward, and the other passenger looked hardly less anxious. They were now upon the level terrace, and the storm apparently spending its fury high up and behind them. But in spite of the clearing of the air, he could not but notice that it was singularly dark. What was more singular, the darkness seemed to have risen from below, and to flow in upon them as they descended. A curtain of profound obscurity, darker even than the mountain wall at their side, shut out the horizon and the valley below. But for the temperature, Masterton would have thought a thunderstorm was closing in upon them. An odd feeling of uneasiness crept over him.

A few fitful gusts now came from the obscurity; one of them was accompanied by what seemed a flight of small startled birds crossing the road ahead of them. A second larger and more sustained flight showed his astonished eyes that they were white, and each bird an enormous flake of *snow*! For an instant the air was filled with these disks, shreds, patches,—two or three clinging together,—like the downfall shaken from a tree, striking the leather roof and sides with a dull thud, spattering the road into which they descended with large rosettes that melted away only to be followed by hundreds more that stuck and *stayed*. In five minutes the ground was white with it, the long road gleaming out ahead in the darkness; the roof and sides of the wagon were overlaid with it as with a coating of plaster of Paris; the harness of the horses, and even the reins, stood out over their steaming backs like white trappings. In five minutes more the steaming backs themselves were blanketed with it; the arms and legs of the outside passengers pinioned to the seats with it, and the arms of the driver kept free only by incessant motion. It was no longer snowing; it was "snowballing;" it was an avalanche out of the slopes of the sky. The exhausted horses floundered in it; the clogging wheels dragged in it; the vehicle at last plunged into a billow of it—and stopped.

The bewildered and half blinded passengers hurried out into the road to assist the driver to unship the wheels and fit the steel runners in their axles. But it was too late! By the time the heavy wagon was converted into a sledge, it was deeply imbedded in wet and clinging snow. The narrow, long-handled shovels borrowed from the prospectors' kits were powerless before this heavy, half liquid impediment. At last the driver, with an oath, relinquished the attempt, and, unhitching his horses, collected the passengers and led them forward by a narrower and more sheltered trail toward the next stations now scarce a mile away. The led horses broke a path before them, the snow fell less heavily, but it was nearly an hour before the straggling procession reached the house, and the snow-coated and exhausted passengers huddled and steamed round the red-hot stove in the bar-room. The driver had vanished with his team into the shed; Masterton's fellow passenger on the box-seat, after a few whispered words to the landlord, also disappeared.

"I see you've got Jake Poole with you," said one of the bar-room loungers to Masterton, indicating the passenger who had just left. "I reckon he's here on the same fool business."

Masterton looked his surprise and mystification.

"Jake Poole, the deputy sheriff," repeated the other. "I reckon he's here pretendin' to hunt for Montagu Trixit like the San Francisco detectives that kem up yesterday."

Masterton with difficulty repressed a start. He had heard of Poole, but did not know him by sight. "I don't think I understand," he said coolly.

"I reckon you're a stranger in these parts," returned the lounger, looking at Masterton curiously. "Ef you warn't, ye'd know that about the last man San Francisco or Canada City *wanted* to ketch is Monty Trixit! He knows too much and *they* know it. But they've got to keep up a show chase—a kind o' cirkis-ridin'—up here to satisfy the stockholders. You bet that Jake Poole hez got his orders—they might kill him to shut his mouth, ef they got an excuse—and he made a fight—but he ain't no such fool. No, sir! Why, the sickest man you ever saw was that director that kem up here with a detective when he found that Monty *hadn't* left the State."

"Then he *is* hiding about here?" said Masterton, with assumed calmness.

The man paused, lowered his voice, and said: "I wouldn't swear he wasn't a mile from whar we're talkin' now. Why, they do allow that he's taken a drink at this very bar *since* the news came!—and that thar's a hoss kept handy in the stable already saddled just to tempt him ef he was inclined to scoot."

"That's only a bluff to start him goin' so that they kin shoot him in his tracks," said a bystander.

"That ain't no good ef he has, as they *say* he has, papers stowed away with a friend that would frighten some mighty partickler men out o' their boots," returned the first speaker. "But he's got his spies too, and thar ain't a man that crosses the Divide as ain't spotted by them. The officers brag about havin' put a cordon around the district, and yet they've just found out that he managed to send a telegraphic dispatch from Black Rock station right under their noses. Why, only an hour or so arter the detectives and the news arrived here, thar kem along one o' them emigrant teams from Pike, and the driver said that a smart-lookin' chap in store-clothes had come out of an old prospector's cabin up thar on the rise about a mile away and asked for a newspaper. And the description the teamster gave just fitted Trixit to a T. Well, the information was give so public like that the detectives *had* to make a rush over thar, and b'gosh! although thar wasn't a soul passed them but a file of Chinese coolies, when they got thar they found *nothin'*,—nothin' but them Chinamen cookin' their rice by the roadside."

Masterton smiled carelessly, and walked to the window, as if intent upon the still falling snow. But he had at once grasped the situation that seemed now almost providential for his inexperience and his mission. The man he was seeking was within his possible reach, if the story he had heard was true. The detectives would not be likely to interfere with his plans, for he was the only man who really wished to meet the fugitive. The presence of Poole made him uneasy, though he had never met the man before. Was it barely possible that he was on the same mission on behalf of others? IF what he heard was true, there might be others equally involved with the absconding manager. But then the spies—how could the deputy sheriff elude them, and how could *he*?

He was turning impatiently away from the window when his eye caught sight of a straggling file of Chinamen breasting the storm on their way up the hill. A sudden idea seized him. Perhaps *they* were the spies in question. He remembered the driver's story. A sudden flash of intuition made him now understand the singular way the file of coolies which they met had diverted their course after passing the wagon. They had recognized the deputy on the box. Stay!—there was another Chinaman in the coach; *He* might have given them the signal. He glanced hurriedly around the room for him; he was gone. Perhaps he had already joined the file he had just seen. His only hope was to follow them—but how? and how to do it quietly? The afternoon was waning; it would be three or four hours before the down coach would arrive, from which the driver expected assistance. Now, if ever, was his opportunity.

He made his way through the back door, and found himself among the straw and chips of the stable-yard and woodshed. Still uncertain what to do, he mechanically passed before the long shed which served as temporary stalls for the steaming wagon horses. At the further end, to his surprise, was a tethered mustang ready saddled and bridled—the opportune horse left for the fugitive, according to the lounger's story. Masterton cast a quick glance around the stable; it was deserted by all save the feeding animals.

He was new to adventures of this kind, or he would probably have weighed the possibilities and consequences. He was ordinarily a thoughtful, reflective man, but like most men of intellect, he was also imaginative and superstitious, and this crowning accident of the providential situation in which he found himself was superior to his logic. There would also be a grim irony in his taking this horse for such a purpose. He again looked and listened. There was no one within sight or hearing. He untied the rope from the bit-ring, leaped into the saddle, and emerged cautiously from the shed. The wet snow muffled the sound of the horse's hoofs. Moving round to the rear of the stable so as to bring it between himself and the station, he clapped his heels into the mustang's flanks and dashed into the open.

At first he was confused and bewildered by the half hidden boulders and snow-shrouded bushes that beset the broken ground, and dazzled by the still driving storm. But he knew that they would also divert attention from his flight, and beyond, he could now see a white slope slowly rising before him, near whose crest a few dark spots were crawling in file, like Alpine climbers. They were the Chinamen he was seeking. He had reasoned that when they discovered they were followed they would, in the absence of any chance of signaling through the storm, detach one of their number to give the alarm. *Him* he would follow. He felt his revolver safe on his hip; he would use it only if necessary to intimidate the spies.

For some moments his ascent through the wet snow was slow and difficult, but as he advanced, he felt a change of temperature corresponding to that he had experienced that afternoon on the wagon coming down. The air grew keener, the snow drier and finer. He kept a sharp lookout for the moving figures, and scanned the horizon for some indication of the prospector's deserted hut. Suddenly the line of figures he was watching seemed to be broken, and then gathered together as a group. Had they detected him? Evidently they had, for, as he had expected, one of them had been detached, and was now moving at right angles from the party towards the right. With a thrill of excitement he urged his horse forward; the group was far to the left, and he was nearing the solitary figure. But to his astonishment, as he approached the top of the slope he now observed another figure, as far to the left of the group as he was to the right, and that figure he could see, even at that distance, was *not* a Chinaman. He halted for a better observation; for an instant he thought it might be the fugitive himself, but as quickly he recognized it was another man—the deputy. It was *he* whom the Chinaman had discovered; it was *he* who had caused the diversion and the dispatch of the vedette to warn the fugitive. His own figure had evidently not yet been detected. His heart beat high with hope; he again dashed forward after the flying messenger, who was undoubtedly seeking the prospector's ruined hut and—Trixit.

But it was no easy matter. At this elevation the snow had formed a crust, over which the single Chinaman—a lithe young figure—skimmed like a skater, while Masterton's horse crashed though it into unexpected depths. Again, the runner could deviate by a shorter cut, while the horseman was condemned to the one half obliterated trail. The only thing in Masterton's favor, however, was that he was steadily increasing his distance from the group and the deputy sheriff, and so cutting off their connection with the messenger. But the trail grew more and more indistinct as it neared the summit, until at last it utterly vanished. Still he kept up his speed toward the active little figure—which now seemed to be that of a mere boy—skimming over the frozen snow. Twice a stumble and flounder of the mustang through the broken crust ought to have warned him of his recklessness, but now a distinct glimpse of a low, blackened shanty, the prospector's ruined hut, toward which the messenger was making, made him forget all else. The distance was lessening between them; he could see the long pigtail of the fugitive standing out from his bent head, when suddenly his horse plunged forward and downward. In an awful instant of suspense and twilight, such as he might have seen in a dream, he felt himself pitched headlong into suffocating depths, followed by a shock, the crushing weight and steaming flank of his horse across his shoulder, utter darkness, and—merciful unconsciousness.

How long he lay there thus he never knew. With his returning consciousness came this strange twilight again,—the twilight of a dream. He was sitting in the new church at Canada City, as he had sat the first Sunday of his arrival there, gazing at the pretty face of Cissy Trixit in the pew opposite him, and wondering who she was. Again he saw the startled, awakened light that came into her adorable eyes, the faint blush that suffused her cheek as she met his inquiring gaze, and the conscious, half conceited, half girlish toss of her little head as she turned her eyes away, and then a file of brown Chinamen, muttering some harsh, uncouth gibberish, interposed between them. This was followed by what seemed to be the crashing in of the church roof, a stifling heat succeeded by a long, deadly chill. But he knew that *this* last was all a dream, and he tried to struggle to his feet to see Cissy's face again,—a reality that he felt would take him out of this horrible trance,—and he called to her across the pew and heard her sweet voice again in answer, and then a wave of unconsciousness once more submerged him.

He came back to life with a sharp tingling of his whole frame as if pierced with a thousand needles.

He knew he was being rubbed, and in his attempts to throw his torturers aside, he saw faintly by the light of a flickering fire that they were Chinamen, and he was lying on the floor of a rude hut. With his first movements they ceased, and, wrapping him like a mummy in warm blankets, dragged him out of the heap of loose snow with which they had been rubbing him, toward the fire that glowed upon the large adobe hearth. The stinging pain was succeeded by a warm glow; a pleasant languor, which made even thought a burden, came over him, and yet his perceptions were keenly alive to his surroundings. He heard the Chinamen mutter something and then depart, leaving him alone. But presently he was aware of another figure that had entered, and was now sitting with its back to him at a rude table, roughly extemporized from a packing-box, apparently engaged in writing. It was a small Chinaman, evidently the one he had chased! The events of the past few hours—his mission, his intentions, and every incident of the pursuit—flashed back upon him. Where was he? What was he doing here? Had Trixit escaped him?

In his exhausted state he was unable to formulate a question which even then he doubted if the Chinaman could understand. So he simply watched him lazily, and with a certain kind of fascination, until he should finish his writing and turn round. His long pigtail, which seemed ridiculously disproportionate to his size,—the pigtail which he remembered had streamed into the air in his flight,—had partly escaped from the discovered hat under which it had been coiled. But what was singular, it was not the wiry black pigtail of his Mongolian fellows, but soft and silky, and as the firelight played upon it, it seemed of a shining chestnut brown! It was like—like—he stopped—was he dreaming again? A long sigh escaped him.

The figure instantly turned. He started. It was Cissy Trixit! There was no mistaking that charming, sensitive face, glowing with health and excitement, albeit showing here and there the mark of the pigment with which it had been stained, now hurriedly washed off. A little of it had run into the corners of her eyelids, and enhanced the brilliancy of her eyes.

He found his tongue with an effort. "What are you doing here?" he asked with a faint voice, and a fainter attempt to smile.

"That's what I might ask about you," she said pertly, but with a slight touch of scorn; "but I guess I know as well as I do about the others. I came here to see my father," she added defiantly.

"And you are the—the—one—I chased?"

"Yes; and I'd have outrun you easily, even with your horse to help you," she said proudly, "only I turned back when you went down into that prospector's hole with your horse and his broken neck atop of you."

He groaned slightly, but more from shame than pain. The young girl took up a glass of whiskey ready on the table and brought it to him. "Take that; it will fetch you all right in a moment. Popper says no bones are broken."

Masterton waived the proffered glass. "Your father—is he here?" he asked hurriedly, recalling his mission.

"Not now; he's gone to the station—to—fetch—my clothes," she said, with a little laugh.

"To the station?" repeated Masterton, bewildered.

"Yes," she replied, "to the station. Of course you don't know the news," she added, with an air of girlish importance. "They've stopped all proceedings against him, and he's as free as you are."

Masterton tried to rise, but another groan escaped him. He was really in pain. Cissy's bright eyes softened. She knelt beside him, her soft breath fanning his hair, and lifted him gently to a sitting position.

"Oh, I've done it before," she laughed, as she read his wonder, with his gratitude, in his eyes. "The horse was already stiff, and you were nearly so, by the time I came up to you and got"—she laughed again—"the *other* Chinaman to help me pull you out of that hole."

"I know I owe you my life," he said, his face flushing.

"It was lucky I was there," she returned naively; "perhaps lucky you were chasing me."

"I'm afraid that of the many who would run after you I should be the least lucky," he said, with an attempt to laugh that did not, however, conceal his mortification; "but I assure you that I only wished to have an interview with your father,—a *business* interview, perhaps as much in his interest as my own."

The old look of audacity came back to her face. "I guess that's what they all came here for, except one, but it didn't keep them from believing and saying he was a thief behind his back. Yet they all wanted his—confidence," she added bitterly.

Masterton felt that his burning cheeks were confessing the truth of this. "You excepted one," he said hesitatingly.

"Yes—the deputy sheriff. He came to help *me*."

"You!"

"Yes, *me*!" A coquettish little toss of her head added to his confusion. "He threw up his job just to follow me, without my knowing it, to see that I didn't come to any harm. He saw me only once, too, at the house when he came to take possession. He said he thought I was 'clear grit' to risk everything to find father, and he said he saw it in me when he was there; that's how he guessed where I was gone when I ran away, and followed me."

"He was as right as he was lucky," said Masterton gravely. "But how did you get here?"

She slipped down on the floor beside him with an unconscious movement that her masculine garments only made the more quaintly girlish, and, clasping her knee with both hands, looked at the fire as she rocked herself slightly backward and forward as she spoke.

"It will shock a proper man like you, I know," she began demurely, "but I came *alone*, with only a Chinaman to guide me. I got these clothes from our laundryman, so that I shouldn't attract attention. I would have got a Chinese lady's dress, but I couldn't walk in *their* shoes,"—she looked down at her little feet encased in wooden sandals,—"and I had a long way to walk. But even if I didn't look quite right to China-men, no white man was able to detect the difference. You passed me twice in the stage, and you didn't know me. I traveled night and day, most of the time walk-ing, and being passed along from one Chinaman to another, or, when we were alone, being slung on a pole between two coolies like a bale of goods. I ate what they could give me, for I dared not go into a shop or a restaurant; I couldn't shut my eyes in their dens, so I stayed awake all night. Yet I got ahead of you and the sheriff,—though I didn't know at the time what *you* were after," she added presently.

He was overcome with wondering admiration of her courage, and of self-reproach at his own short-sightedness. This was the girl he had looked upon as a spoiled village beauty, satisfied with her small triumphs and provincial elevation, and vacant of all other purpose. Here was she—the all-unconscious heroine—and he her critic helpless at her feet! It was not a cheerful reflection, and yet he took a certain delight in his expiation. Perhaps he had half believed in her without knowing it. What could he do or say? I regret to say he dodged the question meanly.

"And you think your disguise escaped detection?" he said, looking markedly at her escaped braid of hair.

She followed his eyes rather than his words, half pettishly caught up the loosened braid, swiftly coiled it around the top of her head, and, clapping the weather-beaten and battered conical hat back again upon it, defiantly said: "Yes! Everybody isn't as critical as you are, and even you wouldn't be—of a Chinaman!"

He had never seen her except when she was arrayed with the full intention to affect the beholders and perfectly conscious of her attractions; he was utterly unprepared for this complete ignoring of adornment now, albeit he was for the first time aware how her real prettiness made it unnecessary. She looked fully as charming in this grotesque head-covering as she had in that paragon of fashion, the new hat, which had excited his tolerant amusement.

"I'm afraid I'm a very poor critic," he said bluntly. "I never conceived that this sort of thing was at all to your taste."

"I came to see my father because I wanted to," she said, with equal bluntness.

"And I came to see him though *I didn't* want to," he said, with a cynical laugh.

She turned, and fixed her brown eyes inquiringly upon him.

"Why did you come, then?"

"I was ordered by my directors."

"Then you did not believe he was a thief?" she asked, her eyes softening.

"It would ill become me to accuse your father or my directors," he answered diplomatically.

She was quick enough to detect the suggestion of moral superiority in his tone, but woman enough to forgive it. "You're no friend of Windibrook," she said, "I know."

"I am not," he replied frankly.

"If you would like to see my popper, I can manage it," she said hesitatingly. "He'll do anything for me," she added, with a touch of her old pride.

"Who could blame him?" returned Masterton gravely. "But if he is a free man now, and able to go where he likes, and to see whom he likes, he may not care to give an audience to a mere messenger."

"You wait and let me see him first," said the girl quickly. Then, as the sound of sleigh-bells came from the road outside, she added, "Here he is. I'll get your clothes; they are out here drying by the fire in the shed." She disappeared through a back door, and returned presently bearing his dried garments. "Dress yourself while I take popper into the shed," she said quickly, and ran out into the road.

Masterton dressed himself with difficulty. Although circulation was now restored, and he felt a glow through his warmed clothes, he had been sorely bruised and shaken by his fall. He had scarcely finished dressing when Montagu Trixit entered from the shed. Masterton looked at him with a new interest and a respect he had never felt before. There certainly was little of the daughter in this keen-faced, resolute-lipped man, though his brown eyes, like hers, had the same frank, steadfast audacity. With a business brevity that was hurried but not unkindly, he hoped Masterton had fully recovered.

"Thanks to your daughter, I'm all right now," said Masterton. "I need not tell you that I believe I owe my life to her energy and courage, for I think you have experienced what she can do in that way. But *you* have had the advantage of those who have only enjoyed her social acquaintance in knowing all the time what she was capable of," he added significantly.

"She is a good girl," said Trixit briefly, yet with a slight rise in color on his dark, sallow cheek, and a sudden wavering of his steadfast eyes. "She tells me you have a message from your directors. I think I know what it is, but we won't discuss it now. As I am going directly to Sacramento, I shall not see them, but I will give you an answer to take to them when we reach the station. I am going to give you a lift there when my daughter is ready. And here she is."

It was the old Cissy that stepped into the room, dressed as she was when she left her father's house two days before. Oddly enough, he fancied that something of her old conscious manner had returned with her clothes, and as he stepped with her into the back seat of the covered sleigh in waiting, he could not help saying, "I really think I understand you better in your other clothes."

A slight blush mounted to Cissy's cheek, but her eyes were still audacious. "All the same, I don't think you'd like to walk down Main Street with me in that rig, although you once thought nothing of taking me over your old mill in your blue blouse and overalls." And having apparently greatly relieved her proud little heart by this enigmatic statement, she grew so chatty and confidential that the young man was satisfied that he had been in love with her from the first!

When they reached the station, Trixit drew him aside. Taking an envelope marked "Private Contracts" from his pocket, he opened it and displayed some papers. "These are the securities. Tell your directors that you have seen them safe in my hands, and that no one else has seen them. Tell them that if they will send me their renewed notes, dated from to-day, to Sacramento within the next three days, I will return the securities. That is my message."

The young man bowed. But before the coach started he managed to draw near to Cissy. "You are not returning to Canada City," he said.

The young girl made a gesture of indignation. "No! I am never going there again. I go with my popper to Sacramento."

"Then I suppose I must say 'good-by.'"

The girl looked at him in surprise. "Popper says you are coming to Sacramento in three days!"

"Am I?"

He looked at her fixedly. She returned his glance audaciously, steadfastly.

"You are," she said, in her low but distinct voice.

"I will."

And he did.

What Happened at the Fonda

PART I

"Well!" said the editor of the "Mountain Clarion," looking up impatiently from his copy. "What's the matter now?"

The intruder in his sanctum was his foreman. He was also acting as pressman, as might be seen from his shirt-sleeves spattered with ink, rolled up over the arm that had just been working "the Archimedian lever that moves the world," which was the editor's favorite allusion to the hand-press that strict economy obliged the "Clarion" to use. His braces, slipped from his shoulders during his work, were looped negligently on either side, their functions being replaced by one hand, which occasionally hitched up his trousers to a securer position. A pair of down-at-heel slippers—dear to the country printer—completed his negligee.

But the editor knew that the ink-spattered arm was sinewy and ready, that a stout and loyal heart beat under the soiled shirt, and that the slipshod slippers did not prevent its owner's foot from being "put down" very firmly on occasion. He accordingly met the shrewd, good-humored blue eyes of his faithful henchman with an interrogating smile.

"I won't keep you long," said the foreman, glancing at the editor's copy with his habitual half humorous toleration of that work, it being his general conviction that news and advertisements were the only valuable features of a newspaper; "I only wanted to talk to you a minute about makin' suthin more o' this yer accident to Colonel Starbottle."

"Well, we've a full report of it in, haven't we?" said the editor wonderingly. "I have even made an editorial para. about the frequency of these accidents, and called attention to the danger of riding those half broken Spanish mustangs."

"yes, ye did that," said the foreman tolerantly; "but ye see, thar's some folks around here that allow it warn't no accident. there's a heap of them believe that no runaway hoss ever mauled the colonel ez *he* got mauled."

"But I heard it from the colonel's own lips," said the editor, "and *he* surely ought to know."

"He mout know and he moutn't, and if he *did* know, he wouldn't tell," said the foreman musingly, rubbing his chin with the cleaner side of his arm. "Ye didn't see him when he was picked up, did ye?"

"No," said the editor. "Only after the doctor had attended him. Why?"

"Jake Parmlee, ez picked him up outer the ditch, says that he was half choked, and his black silk neckhandkercher was pulled tight around his throat. There was a mark on his nose ez ef some one had tried to gouge out his eye, and his left ear was chawed ez ef he'd bin down in a reg'lar rough-and-tumble clinch."

"He told me his horse bolted, buck-jumped, threw him, and he lost consciousness," said the editor positively. "He had no reason for lying, and a man like Starbottle, who carries a Derringer and is a dead shot, would have left his mark on somebody if he'd been attacked."

"That's what the boys say is just the reason why he lied. He was *took suddent*, don't ye see,—he'd no show—and don't like to confess it. See? A man like *him* ain't goin' to advertise that he kin be tackled and left senseless and no one else got hurt by it! His political influence would be ruined here!"

The editor was momentarily staggered at this large truth.

"Nonsense!" he said, with a laugh. "Who would attack Colonel Starbottle in that fashion? He might have been shot on sight by some political enemy with whom he had quarreled—but not *beaten*."

"S'pose it warn't no political enemy?" said the foreman doggedly.

"Then who else could it be?" demanded the editor impatiently.

"That's jest for the press to find out and expose," returned the foreman, with a significant glance at the editor's desk. "I reckon that's whar the 'Clarion' ought to come in."

"In a matter of this kind," said the editor promptly, "the paper has no business to interfere with a man's statement. The colonel has a perfect right to his own secret—if there is one, which I very much doubt. But," he added, in laughing recognition of the half reproachful, half humorous discontent on the foreman's face, "what dreadful theory have *you* and the boys got about it—and what do *you* expect to expose?"

"Well," said the foreman very seriously, "it's jest this: You see, the colonel is mighty sweet on that Spanish woman Ramierez up on the hill yonder. It was her mustang he was ridin' when the row happened near her house."

"Well?" said the editor, with disconcerting placidity.

"Well,"—hesitated the foreman, "you see, they're a bad lot, those Greasers, especially the Ramierez, her husband."

The editor knew that the foreman was only echoing the provincial prejudice against this race, which he himself had always combated. Ramierez kept a fonda or hostelry on a small estate,—the last of many leagues formerly owned by the Spanish grantee, his landlord,—and had a wife of some small coquetries and redundant charms. Gambling took place at the fonda, and it was said the common prejudice against the Mexican did not, however, prevent the American from trying to win his money.

"Then you think Ramierez was jealous of the colonel? But in that case he would have knifed him,—Spanish fashion,—and not without a struggle."

"There's more ways they have o' killin' a man than

that; he might hev been dragged off his horse by a lasso and choked," said the foreman darkly.

The editor had heard of this vaquero method of putting an enemy hors de combat; but it was a clumsy performance for the public road, and the brutality of its manner would have justified the colonel in exposing it.

The foreman saw the incredulity expressed in his face, and said somewhat aggressively, "Of course I know ye don't take no stock in what's said agin the Greasers, and that's what the boys know, and what they said, and that's the reason why I thought I oughter tell ye, so that ye mightn't seem to be always favorin' 'em."

The editor's face darkened slightly, but he kept his temper and his good humor. "So that to prove that the 'Clarion' is unbiased where the Mexicans are concerned, I ought to make it their only accuser, and cast a doubt on the American's veracity?" he said, with a smile.

"I don't mean that," said the foreman, reddening. "Only I thought ye might—as ye understand these folks' ways—ye might be able to get at them easy, and mebbe make some copy outer the blamed thing. It would just make a stir here, and be a big boom for the 'Clarion.'"

"I've no doubt it would," said the editor dryly. "However, I'll make some inquiries; but you might as well let 'the boys' know that the 'Clarion' will not publish the colonel's secret without his permission. Meanwhile," he continued, smiling, "if you are very anxious to add the functions of a reporter to your other duties and bring me any discoveries you may make, I'll—look over your copy."

He good humoredly nodded, and took up his pen again,—a hint at which the embarrassed foreman, under cover of hitching up his trousers, awkwardly and reluctantly withdrew.

It was with some natural youthful curiosity, but no lack of loyalty to Colonel Starbottle, that the editor that evening sought this "war-horse of the Democracy," as he was familiarly known, in his invalid chamber at the Palmetto Hotel. He found the hero with a bandaged ear and—perhaps it was fancy suggested by the story of the choking—cheeks more than usually suffused and apoplectic. Nevertheless, he was seated by the table with a mint julep before him, and welcomed the editor by instantly ordering another.

The editor was glad to find him so much better.

"Gad, sir, no bones broken, but a good deal of 'possum scratching about the head for such a little throw like that. I must have slid a yard or two on my left ear before I brought up."

"You were unconscious from the fall, I believe."

"Only for an instant, sir—a single instant! I recovered myself with the assistance of a No'the'n gentleman—a Mr. Parmlee—who was passing."

"Then you think your injuries were entirely due to your fall?"

The colonel paused with the mint julep halfway to his lips, and set it down. "Sir!" he ejaculated, with astounded indignation.

"You say you were unconscious," returned the editor lightly, "and some of your friends think the injuries inconsistent with what you believe to be the cause. They are concerned lest you were unknowingly the victim of some foul play."

"Unknowingly! Sir! Do you take me for a chuckle-headed niggah, that I don't know when I'm thrown from a buck-jumping mustang? or do they think I'm a Chinaman to be hustled and beaten by a gang of bullies? Do they know, sir, that the account I have given I am responsible for, sir?—personally responsible?"

There was no doubt to the editor that the colonel was perfectly serious, and that the indignation arose from no guilty consciousness of a secret. A man as peppery as the colonel would have been equally alert in defense.

"They feared that you might have been ill used by some evilly disposed person during your unconsciousness," explained the editor diplomatically; "but as you say *that* was only for a moment, and that you were aware of everything that happened"—He paused.

"Perfectly, sir! Perfectly! As plain as I see this julep before me. I had just left the Ramierez rancho. The senora,—a devilish pretty woman, sir,—after a little playful badinage, had offered to lend me her daughter's mustang if I could ride it home. You know what it is, Mr. Grey," he said gallantly. "I'm an older man than you, sir, but a challenge from a d—d fascinating creature, I trust, sir, I am not yet old enough to decline. Gad, sir, I mounted the brute. I've ridden Morgan stock and Blue Grass thoroughbreds bareback, sir, but I've never thrown my leg over such a blanked Chinese cracker before. After he bolted I held my own fairly, but he buck-jumped before I could lock my spurs under him, and the second jump landed me!"

"How far from the Ramierez fonda were you when you were thrown?"

"A matter of four or five hundred yards, sir."

"Then your accident might have been seen from the fonda?"

"Scarcely, sir. For in that case, I may say, without vanity, that—er—the—er senora would have come to my assistance."

"But not her husband?"

The old-fashioned shirt-frill which the colonel habitually wore grew erectile with a swelling indignation, possibly half assumed to conceal a certain conscious satisfaction beneath. "Mr. Grey," he said, with pained severity, "as a personal friend of mine, and a representative of the press,—a power which I respect,—I overlook a disparaging reflection upon a lady, which I can only attribute to the levity of youth and thoughtlessness. At the same time, sir," he added, with illogical sequence, "if Ramierez felt aggrieved at my attentions, he knew where I could be found, sir, and that it was not my habit to decline giving gentlemen—of any nationality—satisfaction—sir!—personal satisfaction."

He paused, and then added, with a singular blending of anxiety and a certain natural dignity, "I trust, sir, that nothing of this—er—kind will appear in your paper."

"It was to keep it out by learning the truth from you, my dear colonel," said the editor lightly, "that I called to-day. Why, it was even suggested," he added, with a laugh, "that you were half strangled by a lasso."

To his surprise the colonel did not join in the laugh, but brought his hand to his loose cravat with an uneasy gesture and a somewhat disturbed face.

"I admit, sir," he said, with a forced smile, "that I experienced a certain sensation of choking, and I may have mentioned it to Mr. Parmlee; but it was due, I believe, sir, to my cravat, which I always wear loosely, as you perceive, becoming twisted in my fall, and in rolling over."

He extended his fat white hand to the editor, who shook it cordially, and then withdrew. Nevertheless, although perfectly satisfied with his mission, and firmly resolved to prevent any further discussion on the subject, Mr. Grey's curiosity was not wholly appeased. What were the relations of the colonel with the Ramierez family? From what he himself had said, the theory of the foreman as to the motives of the attack might have been possible, and the assault itself committed while the colonel was unconscious.

Mr. Grey, however, kept this to himself, briefly told his foreman that he found no reason to add to the account already in type, and dismissed the subject from his mind. The colonel left the town the next day.

One morning a week afterward, the foreman entered the sanctum cautiously, and, closing the door of the composing-room behind him, stood for a moment before the editor with a singular combination of irresolution, shamefacedness, and humorous discomfiture in his face.

Answering the editor's look of inquiry, he began slowly, "Mebbe ye remember when we was talkin' last week o' Colonel Starbottle's accident, I sorter allowed that he knew all the time *why* he was attacked that way, only he wouldn't tell."

"Yes, I remember you were incredulous," said the editor, smiling.

"Well, I take it all back! I reckon he told all he knew. I was wrong! I cave!"

"Why?" asked the editor wonderingly.

"Well, I have been through the mill myself!"

He unbuttoned his shirt collar, pointed to his neck, which showed a slight abrasion and a small livid mark of strangulation at the throat, and added, with a grim smile, "And I've got about as much proof as I want."

The editor put down his pen and stared at him.

"You see, Mr. Grey, it was partly your fault! When you bedeviled me about gettin' that news, and allowed I might try my hand at reportin', I was fool enough to take up the challenge. So once or twice, when I was off duty here, I hung around the Ramierez shanty. Once I went in thar when they were gamblin'; thar war one or two Americans thar that war winnin' as far as I could see, and was pretty full o' that aguardiente that they sell thar—that kills at forty rods. You see, I had a kind o' suspicion that ef thar was any foul play goin' on it might be worked on these fellers *arter* they were drunk, and war goin' home with thar winnin's."

"So you gave up your theory of the colonel being attacked from jealousy?" said the editor, smiling.

"Hol' on! I ain't through yet! I only reckoned that ef thar was a gang of roughs kept thar on the premises they might be used for that purpose, and I only wanted to ketch em at thar work. So I jest meandered into the road when they war about comin' out, and kept my eye skinned for what might happen. Thar was a kind o' corral about a hundred yards down the road, half adobe wall, and a stockade o' palm's on top of it, about six feet high. Some of the palm's were off, and I peeped through, but thar warn't nobody thar. I stood thar, alongside the bank, leanin' my back agin one o' them openin's, and jest watched and waited.

"All of a suddent I felt myself grabbed by my coat collar behind, and my neck-handkercher and collar drawn tight around my throat till I couldn't breathe. The more I twisted round, the tighter the clinch seemed to get. I couldn't holler nor speak, but thar I stood with my mouth open, pinned back agin that cursed stockade, and my arms and legs movin' up and down, like one o' them dancin' jacks! It seems funny,

Mr. Grey—I reckon I looked like a darned fool—but I don't wanter feel ag'in as I did jest then. The clinch o' my throat got tighter; everything got black about me; I was jest goin' off and kalkilatin' it was about time for you to advertise for another foreman, when suthin broke—fetched away!

"It was my collar button, and I dropped like a shot. It was a minute before I could get my breath ag'in, and when I did and managed to climb that darned stockade, and drop on the other side, thar warn't a soul to be seen! A few hosses that stampeded in my gettin' over the fence war all that was there! I was mighty shook up, you bet!—and to make the hull thing perfectly ridic'lous, when I got back to the road, after all I'd got through, darn my skin, ef thar warn't that pesky lot o' drunken men staggerin' along, jinglin' the scads they had won, and enjoyin' themselves, and nobody a-followin' 'em! I jined 'em jest for kempany's sake, till we got back to town, but nothin' happened."

"But, my dear Richards," said the editor warmly, "this is no longer a matter of mere reporting, but of business for the police. You must see the deputy sheriff at once, and bring your complaint—or shall I? It's no joking matter."

"Hol' on, Mr. Grey," replied Richards slowly. "I've told this to nobody but you—nor am I goin' to—sabe? It's an affair of my own—and I reckon I kin take care of it without goin' to the Revised Statutes of the State of California, or callin' out the sheriff's posse."

His humorous blue eyes just then had certain steely points in them like glittering facets as he turned them away, which the editor had seen before on momentous occasions, and he was speaking slowly and composedly, which the editor also knew boded no good to an adversary.

"Don't be a fool, Richards," he said quietly. "Don't take as a personal affront what was a common, vulgar crime. You would undoubtedly have been robbed by that rascal had not the others come along."

Richards shook his head. "I might hev bin robbed a dozen times afore *they* came along—ef that was the little game. No, Mr. Grey,—it warn't no robbery."

"Had you been paying court to the Senora Ramierez, like Colonel Starbottle?" asked the editor, with a smile.

"Not much," returned Richards scornfully; "she ain't my style. But"—he hesitated, and then added, "thar was a mighty purty gal thar—and her darter, I reckon—a reg'lar pink fairy! She kem in only a minute, and they sorter hustled her out ag'in—for darn my skin ef she didn't look as much out o' place in that smoky old garlic-smellin' room as an angel at a bull-fight. And what got me—she was ez white ez you or me, with blue eyes, and a lot o' dark reddish hair in a long braid down her back. Why, only for her purty sing-song voice and her 'Gracias, senor,' you'd hev reckoned she was a Blue Grass girl jest fresh from across the plains."

A little amused at his foreman's enthusiasm, Mr. Grey gave an ostentatious whistle and said, "Come, now, Richards, look here! Really!"

"Only a little girl—a mere child, Mr. Grey—not more'n fourteen if a day," responded Richards, in embarrassed depreciation.

"Yes, but those people marry at twelve," said the editor, with a laugh. "Look out! Your appreciation may have been noticed by some other admirer."

He half regretted this speech the next moment in the quick flush—the male instinct of rivalry—that brought back the glitter of Richards's eyes. "I reckon I kin take care of that, sir," he said slowly, "and I kalkilate that the next time I meet that chap—whoever he may be—he won't see so much of my back as he did."

The editor knew there was little doubt of this, and for an instant believed it his duty to put the matter in the hands of the police. Richards was too good and brave a man to be risked in a bar-room fight. But reflecting that this might precipitate the scandal he wished to avoid, he concluded to make some personal investigation. A stronger curiosity than he had felt before was possessing him. It was singular, too, that Richards's description of the girl was that of a different and superior type—the hidalgo, or fair-skinned Spanish settler. If this was true, what was she doing there—and what were her relations to the Ramierez?

PART II

The next afternoon he went to the fonda. Situated on the outskirts of the town which had long outgrown it, it still bore traces of its former importance as a hacienda, or smaller farm, of one of the old Spanish landholders. The patio, or central courtyard, still existed as a stable-yard for carts, and even one or two horses were tethered to the railings of the inner corridor, which now served as an open veranda to the fonda or inn. The opposite wing was utilized as a tienda, or general shop,—a magazine for such goods as were used by the Mexican inhabitants,—and belonged also to Ramierez.

Ramierez himself—round-whiskered and Sancho Panza-like in build—welcomed the editor with fat, perfunctory urbanity. The fonda and all it contained was at his disposicion.

The senora coquettishly bewailed, in rising and falling inflections, his long absence, his infidelity and general perfidiousness. Truly he was growing great in writing of the affairs of his nation—he could no longer see his humble friends! Yet not long ago—truly that very week—there was the head impresor of Don Pancho's imprenta himself who had been there!

A great man, of a certainty, and they must take what they could get! They were only poor innkeepers; when the governor came not they must welcome the alcalde. To which the editor—otherwise Don Pancho—replied with equal effusion. He had indeed recommended the fonda to his impresor, who was but a courier before him. But what was this? The impresor had been ravished at the sight of a beautiful girl—a mere muchacha—yet of a beauty that deprived the senses—this angel—clearly the daughter of his friend! Here was the old miracle of the orange in full fruition and the lovely fragrant blossom all on the same tree—at the fonda. And this had been kept from him!

"Yes, it was but a thing of yesterday," said the senora, obviously pleased. "The muchacha—for she was but that—had just returned from the convent at San Jose, where she had been for four years. Ah! what would you? The fonda was no place for the child, who should know only the litany of the Virgin—and they had kept her there. And now—that she was home again—she cared only for the horse. From morning to night! Caballeros might come and go! There might be a festival—all the same to her, it made nothing if she had the horse to ride! Even now she was with one in the fields. Would Don Pancho attend and see Cota and her horse?"

The editor smilingly assented, and accompanied his hostess along the corridor to a few steps which brought them to the level of the open meadows of the old farm inclosure. A slight white figure on horseback was careering in the distance. At a signal from Senora Ramierez it wheeled and came down rapidly towards them. But when within a hundred yards the horse was suddenly pulled up vaquero fashion, and the little figure leaped off and advanced toward them on foot, leading the horse.

To his surprise, Mr. Grey saw that she had been riding bareback, and from her discreet halt at that distance he half suspected *astride*! His effusive compliments to the mother on this exhibition of skill were sincere, for he was struck by the girl's fearlessness. But when both horse and rider at last stood before him, he was speechless and embarrassed.

For Richards had not exaggerated the girl's charms. She was indeed dangerously pretty, from her tawny little head to her small feet, and her figure, although comparatively diminutive, was perfectly proportioned. Gray eyed and blonde as she was in color, her racial peculiarities were distinct, and only the good-humored and enthusiastic Richards could have likened her to an American girl.

But he was the more astonished in noticing that her mustang was as distinct and peculiar as herself—a mongrel mare of the extraordinary type known as a "pinto," or "calico" horse, mottled in lavender and pink, Arabian in proportions, and half broken! Her greenish gray eyes, in which too much of the white was visible, had, he fancied, a singular similarity of expression to Cota's own!

Utterly confounded, and staring at the girl in her white, many flounced frock, bare head, and tawny braids, as she stood beside this incarnation of equine barbarism, Grey could remember nothing like it outside of a circus.

He stammered a few words of admiration of the mare. Miss Cota threw out her two arms with a graceful gesture and a profound curtsey, and said—

"A la disposicion de le Usted, senor."

Grey was quick to understand the malicious mischief which underlay this formal curtsey and danced in the girl's eyes, and even fancied it shared by the animal itself. But he was a singularly good rider of untrained stock, and rather proud of his prowess. He bowed.

"I accept that I may have the honor of laying the senorita's gift again at her little feet."

But here the burly Ramierez intervened. "Ah, Mother of God! May the devil fly away with all this nonsense! I will have no more of it," he said impatiently to the girl. "Have a care, Don Pancho," he turned to the editor; "it is a trick!"

"One I think I know," said Grey sapiently. The girl looked at him curiously as he managed to edge between her and the mustang, under the pretense of stroking its glossy neck. "I shall keep *my own* spurs," he said to her in a lower voice, pointing to the sharp, small-roweled American spurs he wore, instead of the large, blunt, five-pointed star of the Mexican pattern.

The girl evidently did not understand him then— though she did a moment later! For without attempting to catch hold of the mustang's mane, Grey in a single leap threw himself across its back. The animal, utterly unprepared, was at first stupefied. But by this time her rider had his seat. He felt her sensitive spine arch like a cat's beneath him as she sprang rocket-wise into the air.

But here she was mistaken! Instead of clinging tightly to her flanks with the inner side of his calves, after the old vaquero fashion to which she was accustomed, he dropped his spurred heels into her sides and allowed his body to rise with her spring, and the cruel spur to cut its track upward from her belly almost to her back.

She dropped like a shot, he dexterously withdrawing his spurs, and regaining his seat, jarred but not discomfited. Again she essayed a leap; the spurs again marked its height in a scarifying track along her smooth barrel. She tried a third leap, but this time dropped halfway as she felt the steel scraping her side, and then stood still, trembling. Grey leaped off!

There was a sound of applause from the innkeeper and his wife, assisted by a lounging vaquero in the corridor. Ashamed of his victory, Grey turned apologetically to Cota. To his surprise she glanced indifferently at the trickling sides of her favorite, and only regarded him curiously.

"Ah," she said, drawing in her breath, "you are strong—and you comprehend!"

"It was only a trick for a trick, senorita," he replied, reddening; "let me look after those scratches in the stable," he added, as she was turning away, leading the agitated and excited animal toward a shed in the rear.

He would have taken the riata which she was still holding, but she motioned him to precede her. He did so by a few feet, but he had scarcely reached the stable door before she suddenly caught him roughly by the shoulders, and, shoving him into the entrance, slammed the door upon him.

Amazed and a little indignant, he turned in time to hear a slight sound of scuffling outside, and to see Cota re-enter with a flushed face.

"Pardon, senor," she said quickly, "but I feared she might have kicked you. Rest tranquil, however, for the servant he has taken her away."

She pointed to a slouching peon with a malevolent face, who was angrily driving the mustang toward the corral.

"Consider it no more! I was rude! Santa Maria! I almost threw you, too; but," she added, with a dazzling smile, "you must not punish me as you have her! For you are very strong—and you comprehend."

But Grey did not comprehend, and with a few hurried apologies he managed to escape his fair but uncanny tormentor. Besides, this unlooked-for incident had driven from his mind the more important object of his visit,—the discovery of the assailants of Richards and Colonel Starbottle.

His inquiries of the Ramierez produced no result. Senor Ramierez was not aware of any suspicious loiterers among the frequenters of the fonda, and except from some drunken American or Irish revelers he had been free of disturbance.

Ah! the peon—an old vaquero—was not an angel, truly, but he was dangerous only to the bull and the wild horses—and he was afraid even of Cota! Mr. Grey was fain to ride home empty of information.

He was still more concerned a week later, on returning unexpectedly one afternoon to his sanctum, to hear a musical, childish voice in the composing-room.

It was Cota! She was there, as Richards explained, on his invitation, to view the marvels and mysteries of printing at a time when they would not be likely to "disturb Mr. Grey at his work." But the beaming face of Richards and the simple tenderness of his blue eyes plainly revealed the sudden growth of an evidently sincere passion, and the unwonted splendors of his best clothes showed how carefully he had prepared for the occasion.

Grey was worried and perplexed, believing the girl a malicious flirt. Yet nothing could be more captivating than her simple and childish curiosity, as she watched Richards swing the lever of the press, or stood by his side as he marshaled the type into files on his "composing-stick." He had even printed a card with her name, "Senorita Cota Ramierez," the type of which had been set up, to the accompaniment of ripples of musical laughter, by her little brown fingers.

The editor might have become quite sentimental and poetical had he not noticed that the gray eyes which often rested tentatively and meaningly on himself, even while apparently listening to Richards, were more than ever like the eyes of the mustang on whose scarred flanks her glance had wandered so coldly.

He withdrew presently so as not to interrupt his foreman's innocent tete-a-tete, but it was not very long after that Cota passed him on the highroad with the pinto horse in a gallop, and blew him an audacious kiss from the tips of her fingers.

For several days afterwards Richards's manner was tinged with a certain reserve on the subject of Cota which the editor attributed to the delicacy of a serious affection, but he was surprised also to find that his foreman's eagerness to discuss his unknown assailant had somewhat abated. Further discussion regarding it naturally dropped, and the editor was beginning to lose his curiosity when it was suddenly awakened by a chance incident.

An intimate friend and old companion of his—one Enriquez Saltillo—had diverged from a mountain trip especially to call upon him. Enriquez was a scion of one of the oldest Spanish-California families, and in addition to his friendship for the editor it pleased him also to affect an intense admiration of American ways and habits, and even to combine the current California slang with his native precision of speech—and a certain ironical levity still more his own.

It seemed, therefore, quite natural to Mr. Grey to find him seated with his feet on the editorial desk, his hat cocked on the back of his head, reading the "Clarion" exchanges. But he was up in a moment, and had embraced Grey with characteristic effusion.

"I find myself, my leetle brother, but an hour ago two leagues from this spot! I say to myself, 'Hola! It is the home of Don Pancho—my friend! I shall find him composing the magnificent editorial leader, collecting the subscription of the big pumpkin and the great gooseberry, or gouging out the eye of the rival editor, at which I shall assist!' I hesitate no longer; I fly on the instant, and I am here."

Grey was delighted. Saltillo knew the Spanish population thoroughly—his own superior race and their Mexican and Indian allies. If any one could solve the mystery of the Ramierez fonda, and discover Richards's unknown assailant, it was *he*! But Grey contented himself, at first, with a few brief inquiries concerning the beautiful Cota and her anonymous association with the Ramierez. Enriquez was as briefly communicative.

"Of your suspicions, my leetle brother, you are right—on the half! That leetle angel of a Cota is, without doubt, the daughter of the adorable Senora Ramierez, but not of the admirable senor—her husband. Ah! what would you? We are a simple, patriarchal race; thees Ramierez, he was the Mexican tenant of the old Spanish landlord—such as my father—and we are ever the fathers of the poor, and sometimes of their children. It is possible, therefore, that the exquisite Cota resemble the Spanish landlord. Ah! stop—remain tranquil! I remember," he went on, suddenly striking his forehead with a dramatic gesture, "the old owner of thees ranch was my cousin Tiburcio. Of a consequence, my friend, thees angel is my second cousin! Behold! I shall call there on the instant. I shall embrace my long-lost relation. I shall introduce my best friend, Don Pancho, who lofe her. I shall say, 'Bless you, my children,' and it is feenish! I go! I am gone even now!"

He started up and clapped on his hat, but Grey caught him by the arm.

"For Heaven's sake, Enriquez, be serious for once," he said, forcing him back into the chair. "And don't speak so loud. The foreman in the other room is an enthusiastic admirer of the girl. In fact, it is on his account that I am making these inquiries."

"Ah, the gentleman of the pantuflos, whose trousers will not remain! I have seen him, friend. Truly he has the ambition excessif to arrive from the bed to go to the work without the dress or the wash. But," in recognition of Grey's half serious impatience, "remain tranquil. On him I shall not go back! I have said! The friend of my friend is ever the same as my friend! He is truly not seducing to the eye, but without doubt he will arrive a governor or a senator in good time. I shall gif to him my second cousin. It is feenish! I will tell him now!"

He attempted to rise, but was held down and vigorously shaken by Grey.

"I've half a mind to let you do it, and get chucked through the window for your pains," said the editor, with a half laugh. "Listen to me. This is a more serious matter than you suppose."

And Grey briefly recounted the incident of the mysterious attacks on Starbottle and Richards. As he proceeded he noticed, however, that the ironical light died out of Enriquez's eyes, and a singular thoughtfulness, yet unlike his usual precise gravity, came over his face. He twirled the ends of his penciled mustache—an unfailing sign of Enriquez's emotion.

"The same accident that arrive to two men that shall be as opposite as the gallant Starbottle and the excellent Richards shall not prove that it come from Ramierez, though they both were at the fonda," he said gravely. "The cause of it have not come to-day, nor yesterday, nor last week. The cause of it have arrive before there was any gallant Starbottle or excellent Richards; before there was any American in California—before you and I, my leetle brother, have lif! The cause happen first—*two hundred years ago!*"

The editor's start of impatient incredulity was checked by the unmistakable sincerity of Enriquez's face. "It is so," he went on gravely; "it is an old story—it is a long story. I shall make him short—and new."

He stopped and lit a cigarette without changing his odd expression.

"It was when the padres first have the mission, and take the heathen and convert him—and save his soul. It was their business, you comprehend, my Pancho? The more heathen they convert, the more soul they save, the better business for their mission shop. But the heathen do not always wish to be 'convert;' the heathen fly, the heathen skidaddle, the heathen will not remain, or will backslide. What will you do? So the holy fathers make a little game. You do not of a possibility comprehend how the holy fathers make a convert, my leetle brother?" he added gravely.

"No," said the editor.

"I shall tell to you. They take from the presidio five or six dragons—you comprehend—the cavalry soldiers, and they pursue the heathen from his little hut. When they cannot surround him and he fly, they catch him with the lasso, like the wild hoss. The lasso catch him around the neck; he is obliged to remain. Sometime he is strangle. Sometime he is dead, but the soul is save! You believe not, Pancho? I see you wrinkle the brow—you flash the eye; you like it not? Believe me, I like it not, neither, but it is so!"

He shrugged his shoulders, threw away his half smoked cigarette, and went on.

"One time a padre who have the zeal excessif for the saving of soul, when he find the heathen, who is a young girl, have escape the soldiers, he of himself have seize the lasso and flung it! He is lucky; he catch her—but look you! She stop not—she still fly! She not only fly, but of a surety she drag the good padre with her! He cannot loose himself, for his riata is fast to the saddle; the dragons cannot help, for he is drag so fast. On the instant she have gone—and so have the padre. For why? It is not a young girl he have lasso, but the devil! You comprehend—it is a punishment—a retribution—he is feenish! And forever!

"For every year he must come back a spirit—on a spirit hoss—and swing the lasso, and make as if to catch the heathen. He is condemn ever to play his little game; now there is no heathen more to convert, he catch what he can. My grandfather have once seen him—it is night and a storm, and he pass by like a flash! My grandfather like it not—he is much dissatisfied! My uncle have seen him, too, but he make the sign of the cross, and the lasso have fall to the side, and my uncle have much gratification. A vaquero of my father and a peon of my cousin have both been picked up, lassoed, and dragged dead.

"Many peoples have died of him in the strangling. Sometime he is seen, sometime it is the woman only that one sees—sometime it is but the hoss. But ever somebody is dead—strangle! Of a truth, my friend, the gallant Starbottle and the ambitious Richards have just escaped!"

The editor looked curiously at his friend. There was not the slightest suggestion of mischief or irony in his tone or manner; nothing, indeed, but a sincerity and anxiety usually rare with his temperament. It struck him also that his speech had but little of the odd California slang which was always a part of his imitative levity. He was puzzled.

"Do you mean to say that this superstition is well known?" he asked, after a pause.

"Among my people—yes."

"And do *you* believe in it?"

Enriquez was silent. Then he arose, and shrugged his shoulders. "Quien sabe? It is not more difficult to comprehend than your story."

He gravely put on his hat. With it he seemed to have put on his old levity. "Come, behold, it is a long time between drinks! Let us to the hotel and the barkeep, who shall give up the smash of brandy and the julep of mints before the lasso of Friar Pedro shall prevent us the swallow! Let us skiddadle!"

Mr. Grey returned to the "Clarion" office in a much more satisfied condition of mind. Whatever faith he held in Enriquez's sincerity, for the first time since the attack on Colonel Starbottle he believed he had found a really legitimate journalistic opportunity in the incident. The legend and its singular coincidence with the outrages would make capital "copy."

No names would be mentioned, yet even if Colonel Starbottle recognized his own adventure, he could not possibly object to this interpretation of it. The editor had found that few people objected to be the hero of a ghost story, or the favored witness of a spiritual manifestation. Nor could Richards find fault with this view of his own experience, hitherto kept a secret, so long as it did not refer to his relations with the fair Cota. Summoning him at once to his sanctum, he briefly repeated the story he had just heard, and his purpose of using it. To his surprise, Richards's face assumed a seriousness and anxiety equal to Enriquez's own.

"It's a good story, Mr. Grey," he said awkwardly, "and I ain't sayin' it ain't mighty good newspaper stuff, but it won't do *now*, for the whole mystery's up and the assailant found."

"Found! When? Why didn't you tell me before?" exclaimed Grey, in astonishment.

"I didn't reckon ye were so keen on it," said Richards embarrassedly, "and—and—it wasn't my own secret altogether."

"Go on," said the editor impatiently.

"Well," said Richards slowly and doggedly, "ye see there was a fool that was sweet on Cota, and he allowed himself to be bedeviled by her to ride her cursed pink and yaller mustang. Naturally the beast bolted at once, but he managed to hang on by the mane for half a mile or so, when it took to buck-jumpin'. The first 'buck' threw him clean into the road, but didn't stun him, yet when he tried to rise, the first thing he knowed he was grabbed from behind and half choked by somebody. He was held so tight that he couldn't turn, but he managed to get out his revolver and fire two shots under his arm. The grip held on for a minute, and then loosened, and the somethin' slumped down on top o' him, but he managed to work himself around. And then—what do you think he saw?—why, that thar hoss! with two bullet holes in his neck, lyin' beside him, but still grippin' his coat collar and neck-handkercher in his teeth! Yes, sir! the rough that attacked Colonel Star-bottle, the villain that took me behind when I was leanin' agin that cursed fence, was that same God-forsaken, hell-invented pinto hoss!"

In a flash of recollection the editor remembered his own experience, and the singular scuffle outside the stable door of the fonda. Undoubtedly Cota had saved him from a similar attack.

"But why not tell this story with the other?" said the editor, returning to his first idea. "It's tremendously interesting."

"It won't do," said Richards, with dogged resolution.

"Why?"

"Because, Mr. Grey—that fool was myself!"

"You! Again attacked!"

"Yes," said Richards, with a darkening face. "Again attacked, and by the same hoss! Cota's hoss! Whether Cota was or was not knowin' its tricks, she was actually furious at me for killin' it—and it's all over 'twixt me and her."

"Nonsense," said the editor impulsively; "she will forgive you! You didn't know your assailant was a horse *when you fired*. Look at the attack on you in the road!"

Richards shook his head with dogged hopelessness. "It's no use, Mr. Grey. I oughter guessed it was a hoss then—thar was nothin' else in that corral. No! Cota's already gone away back to San Jose, and I reckon the Ramierez has got scared of her and packed her off. So, on account of its bein' *her* hoss, and what happened betwixt me and her, you see my mouth is shut."

"And the columns of the 'Clarion' too," said the editor, with a sigh.

"I know it's hard, sir, but it's better so. I've reckoned mebbe she was a little crazy, and since you've told me that Spanish yarn, it mout be that she was sort o' playin' she was that priest, and trained that mustang ez she did."

After a pause, something of his old self came back into his blue eyes as he sadly hitched up his braces and passed them over his broad shoulders. "Yes, sir, I was a fool, for we've lost the only bit of real sensation news that ever came in the way of the 'Clarion.'"

A Jack and Jill of the Sierras

It was four o'clock in the afternoon, and the hottest hour of the day on that Sierran foothill. The western sun, streaming down the mile-long slope of close-set pine crests, had been caught on an outlying ledge of glaring white quartz, covered with mining tools and debris, and seemed to have been thrown into an incandescent rage. The air above it shimmered and became visible. A white canvas tent on it was an object not to be borne; the steel-tipped picks and shovels, intolerable to touch and eyesight, and a tilted tin prospecting pan, falling over, flashed out as another sun of insufferable effulgence. At such moments the five members of the "Eureka Mining Company" prudently withdrew to the nearest pine-tree, which cast a shadow so sharply defined on the glistening sand that the impingement of a hand or finger beyond that line cut like a knife. The men lay, or squatted, in this shadow, feverishly puffing their pipes and waiting for the sun to slip beyond the burning ledge. Yet so irritating was the dry air, fragrant with the aroma of the heated pines, that occasionally one would start up and walk about until he had brought on that profuse perspiration which gave a momentary relief, and, as he believed, saved him from sunstroke. Suddenly a voice exclaimed querulously:—

"Derned if the blasted bucket ain't empty ag'in! Not a drop left, by Jimminy!"

A stare of helpless disgust was exchanged by the momentarily uplifted heads; then every man lay down again, as if trying to erase himself.

"Who brought the last?" demanded the foreman.

"I did," said a reflective voice coming from a partner lying comfortably on his back, "and if anybody reckons I'm going to face Tophet ag'in down that slope, he's mistaken!" The speaker was thirsty—but he had principles.

"We must throw round for it," said the foreman, taking the dice from his pocket.

He cast; the lowest number fell to Parkhurst, a florid, full-blooded Texan. "All right, gentlemen," he said, wiping his forehead, and lifting the tin pail with a resigned air, "only *ef* anything comes to me on that bare stretch o' stage road,—and I'm kinder seein' things spotty and black now, remember you ain't anywhar *nearer* the water than you were! I ain't sayin' it for myself—but it mout be rough on *you*—and"—

"Give *me* the pail," interrupted a tall young fellow, rising. "I'll risk it."

Cries of "Good old Ned," and "Hunky boy!" greeted him as he took the pail from the perspiring Parkhurst, who at once lay down again. "You mayn't be a profes-sin' Christian, in good standin', Ned Bray," continued Parkhurst from the ground, "but you're about as white as they make 'em, and you're goin' to do a Heavenly Act! I repeat it, gents—a Heavenly Act!"

Without a reply Bray walked off with the pail, stopping only in the underbrush to pluck a few soft fronds of fern, part of which he put within the crown of his hat, and stuck the rest in its band around the outer brim, making a parasol-like shade above his shoulders. Thus equipped he passed through the outer fringe of pines to a rocky trail which began to descend towards the stage road. Here he was in the full glare of the sun and its reflection from the heated rocks, which scorched his feet and pricked his bent face into a rash. The descent was steep and necessarily slow from the slipperiness of the desic-cated pine needles that had fallen from above. Nor were his troubles over when, a few rods further, he came upon the stage road, which here swept in a sharp curve round the flank of the mountain, its red dust, ground by heavy wagons and pack-trains into a fine powder, was nevertheless so heavy with some metallic substance that it scarcely lifted with the foot, and he was obliged to literally wade through it. Yet there were two hundred yards of this road to be passed before he could reach that point of its bank where a narrow and precipitous trail dropped diago-nally from it, to creep along the mountain side to the spring he was seeking.

When he reached the trail, he paused to take breath and wipe the blinding beads of sweat from his eyes before he cautiously swung himself over the bank into it. A single misstep here would have sent him headlong to the tops of pine-trees a thousand feet below. Holding his pail in one hand, with the other he steadied himself by clutching the ferns and brambles at his side, and at last reached the spring—a niche in the mountain side with a ledge scarcely four feet wide. He had merely accomplished the ordinary gymnastic feat performed by the members of the Eureka Company four or five times a day! But the day was exceptionally hot. He held his wrists to cool their throbbing pulses in the clear, cold stream that gurgled into its rocky basin; he threw the water over his head and shoulders; he swung his legs over the ledge and let the overflow fall on his dusty shoes and ankles. Gentle and delicious rigors came over him. He sat with half closed eyes looking across the dark olive depths of the canyon between him and the opposite mountain. A hawk was swinging lazily above it, apparently within a stone's throw of him; he knew it was at least a mile away. Thirty feet above him ran the stage road; he could hear quite distinctly the slow thud of hoofs, the dull jar of harness, and the labored creaking of the Pioneer Coach as it crawled up the long ascent, part of which he had just passed. He thought of it,—a slow drifting cloud of dust and heat, as he had often seen it, abandoned by even its passengers, who sought shelter in the wayside pines as they toiled behind it to the summit,—and hugged himself in the grateful shadows of the spring. It had passed out of hearing and thought, he had turned to fill his pail, when he was startled by a shower of dust and gravel from the road above, and the next moment he was thrown violently down, blinded and pinned against the ledge by the fall of some heavy body on his back and shoulders. His last flash of consciousness was that he had been struck by a sack of flour slipped from the pack of some passing mule.

How long he remained unconscious he never knew. It was probably not long, for his chilled hands and arms, thrust by the blow on his shoulders into the pool of water, assisted in restoring him. He came to with a sense of suffocating pressure on his back, but his head and shoulders were swathed in utter darkness by the folds of some soft fabrics and draperies, which, to his connecting consciousness, seemed as if the contents of a broken bale or trunk had also fallen from the pack. With a tremendous effort he succeeded in getting his arm out of the pool, and attempted to free his head from its blinding enwrappings. In doing so his hand suddenly touched human flesh—a soft, bared arm! With the same astounding discovery came one more terrible: that arm belonged to the weight that was pressing him down; and now, assisted by his struggles, it was slowly slipping toward the brink of the ledge and the abyss below! With a desperate effort he turned on his side, caught the body,—as such it was,—dragged it back on the ledge, at the same moment that, freeing his head from its covering,—a feminine skirt,—he discovered it was a woman!

She had been also unconscious, although the touch of his cold, wet hand on her skin had probably given her a shock that was now showing itself in a convulsive shudder of her shoulders and a half opening of her eyes. Suddenly she began to stare at him, to draw in her knees and feet toward her, sideways, with a feminine movement, as she smoothed out her skirt, and kept it down with a hand on which she leaned. She was a tall, handsome girl, from what he could judge of her half-sitting figure in her torn silk dust-cloak, which, although its cape and one sleeve were split into ribbons, had still protected her delicate, well-fitting gown beneath. She was evidently a lady.

"What—is it?—what has happened?" she said faintly, yet with a slight touch of formality in her manner.

"You must have fallen—from the road above," said Bray hesitatingly.

"From the road above?" she repeated, with a slight frown, as if to concentrate her thought. She glanced upward, then at the ledge before her, and then, for the first time, at the darkening abyss below. The color, which had begun to return, suddenly left her face here, and she drew instinctively back against the mountain side. "Yes," she half murmured to herself, rather than to him, "it must be so. I was walking too near the bank—and—I fell!" Then turning to him, she said, "And you found me lying here when you came."

"I think," stammered Bray, "that I was here when you fell, and I—I broke the fall." He was sorry for it a moment afterward.

She lifted her handsome gray eyes to him, saw the dust, dirt, and leaves on his back and shoulders, the collar of his shirt torn open, and a few spots of blood from a bruise on his forehead. Her black eyebrows straightened again as she said coldly, "Dear me! I am very sorry; I couldn't help it, you know. I hope you are not otherwise hurt."

"No," he replied quickly. "But you, are you sure you are not injured? It must have been a terrible shock."

"I'm not hurt," she said, helping herself to her feet by the aid of the mountain-side bushes, and ignoring his proffered hand. "But," she added quickly and impressively, glancing upward toward the stage road overhead, "why don't they come? They must have missed me! I must have been here a long time; it's too bad!"

"*They* missed you?" he repeated diffidently.

"Yes," she said impatiently, "of course! I wasn't alone. Don't you understand? I got out of the coach to walk uphill on the bank under the trees. It was so hot and stuffy. My foot must have slipped up there—and—I—slid—down. Have you heard any one calling me? Have you called out yourself?"

Mr. Bray did not like to say he had only just recovered consciousness. He smiled vaguely and foolishly. But on turning around in her impatience, she caught sight of the chasm again, and lapsed quite white against the mountain side.

"Let me give you some water from the spring," he said eagerly, as she sank again to a sitting posture; "it will refresh you."

He looked hesitatingly around him; he had neither cup nor flask, but he filled the pail and held it with great dexterity to her lips. She drank a little, extracted a lace handkerchief from some hidden pocket, dipped its point in the water, and wiped her face delicately, after a certain feline fashion. Then, catching sight of some small object in the fork of a bush above her, she quickly pounced upon it, and with a swift sweep of her hand under her skirt, put on *her fallen slipper*, and stood on her feet again.

"How does one get out of such a place?" she asked fretfully, and then, glancing at him half indignantly, "why don't you shout?"

"I was going to tell you," he said gently, "that when you are a little stronger, we can get out by the way I came in,—along the trail."

He pointed to the narrow pathway along the perilous incline. Somehow, with this tall, beautiful creature beside him, it looked more perilous than before. She may have thought so too, for she drew in her breath sharply and sank down again.

"Is there no other way?"

"None!"

"How did *you* happen to be here?" she asked suddenly, opening her gray eyes upon him. "What did you come here for?" she went on, almost impertinently.

"To fetch a pail of water." He stopped, and then

it suddenly occurred to him that after all there was no reason for his being bullied by this tall, good-looking girl, even if he *had* saved her. He gave a little laugh, and added mischievously, "Just like Jack and Jill, you know."

"What?" she said sharply, bending her black brows at him.

"Jack and Jill," he returned carelessly; "I broke my crown, you know, and *you*,"—he did not finish.

She stared at him, trying to keep her face and her composure; but a smile, that on her imperious lips he thought perfectly adorable, here lifted the corners of her mouth, and she turned her face aside. But the smile, and the line of dazzling little teeth it revealed, were unfortunately on the side toward him. Emboldened by this, he went on, "I couldn't think what had happened. At first I had a sort of idea that part of a mule's pack had fallen on top of me,—blankets, flour, and all that sort of thing, you know, until"—

Her smile had vanished. "Well," she said impatiently, "until?"

"Until I touched you. I'm afraid I gave you a shock; my hand was dripping from the spring."

She colored so quickly that he knew she must have been conscious at the time, and he noticed now that the sleeve of her cloak, which had been half torn off her bare arm, was pinned together over it. When and how had she managed to do it without his detecting the act?

"At all events," she said coldly, "I'm glad you have not received greater injury from—your mule pack."

"I think we've both been very lucky," he said simply.

She did not reply, but remained looking furtively at the narrow trail. Then she listened. "I thought I heard voices," she said, half rising.

"Shall I shout?" he asked.

"No! You say there's no use—there's only this way out of it!"

"I might go up first, and perhaps get assistance—a rope or chair," he suggested.

"And leave me here alone?" she cried, with a horrified glance at the abyss. "No, thank you! I should be over that ledge before you came back! There's a dreadful fascination in it even now. No! I think I'd rather go—at once! I never shall be stronger as long as I stay near it; I may be weaker."

She gave a petulant little shiver, and then, though paler and evidently agitated, composed her tattered and dusty outer garments in a deft, ladylike way, and leaned back against the mountain side, He saw her also glance at his loosened shirt front and hanging neckerchief, and with a heightened color he quickly re-knotted it around his throat. They moved from the ledge toward the trail. Suddenly she started back.

"But it's only wide enough for *one*, and I never—*never*—could even stand on it a minute alone!" she exclaimed.

He looked at her critically. "We will go together, side by side," he said quietly, "but you will have to take the outside."

"Outside!" she repeated, recoiling. "Impossible! I shall fall."

"I shall keep hold of you," he explained; "you need not fear that. Stop! I'll make it safer." He untied the large bandanna silk handkerchief which he wore around his shoulders, knotted one end of it firmly to his belt, and handed her the other.

"Do you think you can hold on to that?"

"I—don't know,"—she hesitated. "If I should fall?"

"Stay a moment! Is your belt strong?" He pointed to a girdle of yellow leather which caught her tunic around her small waist.

"Yes," she said eagerly, "it's real leather."

He gently slipped the edge of the handkerchief under it and knotted it. They were thus linked together by a foot of handkerchief.

"I feel much safer," she said, with a faint smile.

"But if I should fall," he remarked, looking into her eyes, "you would go too! Have you thought of that?"

"Yes." Her previous charming smile returned. "It would be really Jack and Jill this time."

They passed out on the trail. "Now I must take *your* arm," he said laughingly; "not you *mine*." He passed his arm under hers, holding it firmly. It was the one he had touched. For the first few steps her uncertain feet took no hold of the sloping mountain side, which seemed to slip sideways beneath her. He was literally carrying her on his shoulder. But in a few moments she saw how cleverly he balanced himself, always leaning toward the hillside, and presently she was able to help him by a few steps. She expressed her surprise at his skill.

"It's nothing; I carry a pail of water up here without spilling a drop."

She stiffened slightly under this remark, and indeed so far overdid her attempt to walk without his aid, that her foot slipped on a stone, and she fell outward toward the abyss. But in an instant his arm was transferred from her elbow to her waist, and in the momentum of his quick recovery they both landed panting against the mountain side.

"I'm afraid you'd have spilt the pail that time," she said, with a slightly heightened color, as she disengaged herself gently from his arm.

"No," he answered boldly, "for the pail never would have stiffened itself in a tiff, and tried to go alone."

"Of course not, if it were only a pail," she responded.

They moved on again in silence. The trail was growing a little steeper toward the upper end and the road bank. Bray was often himself obliged to seek the friendly aid of a manzanita or thornbush to support them. Suddenly she stopped and caught his arm. "There!" she said. "Listen! They're coming!"

Bray listened; he could hear at intervals a far-off shout; then a nearer one—a name—"Eugenia." So that was *hers*!

"Shall I shout back?" he asked.

"Not yet!" she answered. "Are we near the top?" A sudden glow of pleasure came over him—he knew not why, except that she did not look delighted, excited, or even relieved.

"Only a few yards more," he said, with an unaffected half sigh.

"Then I'd better untie this," she suggested, beginning to fumble at the knot of the handkerchief which linked them.

Their heads were close together, their fingers often met; he would have liked to say something, but he could only add: "Are you sure you will feel quite safe? It is a little steeper as we near the bank."

"You can hold me," she replied simply, with a superbly unconscious lifting of her arm, as she yielded her waist to him again, but without raising her eyes.

He did,—holding her rather tightly, I fear, as they clambered up the remaining slope, for it seemed to him as a last embrace. As he lifted her to the road bank, the shouts came nearer; and glancing up, he saw two men and a woman running down the hill toward them. He turned to Eugenia. In that instant she had slipped the tattered dust-coat from her shoulder, thrown it over her arm, set her hat straight, and was calmly awaiting them with a self-possession and coolness that seemed to shame their excitement. He noticed, too, with the quick perception of unimportant things which comes to some natures at such moments, that she had plucked a sprig of wild myrtle from the mountain side, and was wearing it on her breast.

"Goodness Heavens! Genie! What has happened! Where have you been?"

"Eugenia! this is perfect madness!" began the elder man didactically. "You have alarmed us beyond measure—kept the stage waiting, and now it is gone!"

"Genie! Look here, I say! We've been hunting for you everywhere. What's up?" said the younger man, with brotherly brusqueness.

As these questions were all uttered in the same breath, Eugenia replied to them collectively. "It was so hot that I kept along the bank here, while you were on the other side. I heard the trickle of water somewhere down there, and searching for it my foot slipped. This gentleman"—she indicated Bray—"was on a little sort of a trail there, and assisted me back to the road again."

The two men and the woman turned and stared at Bray with a look of curiosity that changed quickly into a half contemptuous unconcern. They saw a youngish sort of man, with a long mustache, a two days' growth of beard, a not overclean face, that was further streaked with red on the temple, a torn flannel shirt, that showed a very white shoulder beside a sunburnt throat and neck, and soiled white trousers stuck into muddy high boots—in fact, the picture of a broken-down miner. But their unconcern was as speedily changed again into resentment at the perfect ease and equality with which he regarded them, a regard the more exasperating as it was not without a suspicion of his perception of some satire or humor in the situation.

"Ahem! very much obliged, I am sure. I—er"—

"The lady has thanked me," interrupted Bray, with a smile.

"Did you fall far?" said the younger man to Eugenia, ignoring Bray.

"Not far," she answered, with a half appealing look at Bray.

"Only a few feet," added the latter, with prompt mendacity, "just a little slip down."

The three new-comers here turned away, and, surrounding Eugenia, conversed in an undertone. Quite conscious that he was the subject of discussion, Bray lingered only in the hope of catching a parting glance from Eugenia. The words "*you* do it," "No, *you!*" "It would come better from *her*," were distinctly audible to him. To his surprise, however, she suddenly broke through them, and advancing to him, with a dangerous brightness in her beautiful eyes, held out her slim hand. "My father, Mr. Neworth, my brother, Harry Neworth, and my aunt, Mrs. Dobbs," she said, indicating each one with a graceful inclination of her handsome head, "all think I ought to give you something and send you away. I believe that is the way they put it. I think differently! I come to ask you to let me once more thank you for your good service to me to-day—which I shall never forget." When he had returned her firm handclasp for a minute, she coolly rejoined the discomfited group.

"She's no sardine," said Bray to himself emphatically, "but I suspect she'll catch it from her folks for

this. I ought to have gone away at once, like a gentleman, hang it!"

He was even angrily debating with himself whether
he ought not to follow her to protect her from her gesticulating relations as they all trailed up the hill with
her, when he reflected that it would only make mat-
ters worse. And with it came the dreadful reflection
that as yet he had not carried the water to his expect-
ing and thirsty comrades. He had forgotten them for
these lazy, snobbish, purse-proud San Franciscans—
for Bray had the miner's supreme contempt for the
moneyed trading classes. What would the boys think
of him! He flung himself over the bank, and hastened
recklessly down the trail to the spring. But here again
he lingered—the place had become suddenly hal-
lowed. How deserted it looked without her! He gazed
eagerly around on the ledge for any trace that she had
left—a bow, a bit of ribbon, or even a hairpin that had
fallen from her.

As the young man slowly filled the pail he caught
sight of his own reflection in the spring. It certainly
was not that of an Adonis! He laughed honestly; his
sense of humor had saved him from many an extravagance, and mitigated many a disappointment
before this. Well! She was a plucky, handsome girl—
even if she was not for him, and he might never set
eyes on her again. Yet it was a hard pull up that trail
once more, carrying an insensible pail of water in
the hand that had once sustained a lovely girl! He
remembered her reply to his badinage, "Of course

not—if it were only a pail," and found a dozen pretty interpretations of it. Yet he was not in love! No! He was too poor and too level headed for that! And he was unaffectedly and materially tired, too, when he reached the road again, and rested, leaving the spring and its little idyl behind.

By this time the sun had left the burning ledge of the Eureka Company, and the stage road was also in shadow, so that his return through its heavy dust was less difficult. And when he at last reached the camp, he found to his relief that his prolonged absence had been overlooked by his thirsty companions in a larger excitement and disappointment; for it appeared that a well-known San Francisco capitalist, whom the foreman had persuaded to visit their claim with a view to advance and investment, had actually come over from Red Dog for that purpose, and had got as far as the summit when he was stopped by an accident, and delayed so long that he was obliged to go on to Sacramento without making his examination.

"That was only his excuse—mere flap-doodle!" interrupted the pessimistic Jerrold. "He was foolin' you; he'd heard of suthin better! The idea of calling that affair an 'accident,' or one that would stop any man who meant business!"

Bray had become uneasily conscious. "What was the accident?" he asked.

"A d—d fool woman's accident," broke in the misogynist Parkhurst, "and it's true! That's what makes it so cussed mean. For there's allus a woman at the bottom of such things—bet your life! Think of 'em comin' here. Thar ought to be a law agin it."

"But what was it?" persisted Bray, becoming more apprehensive.

"Why, what does that blasted fool of a capitalist do but bring with him his daughter and auntie to 'see the wonderful scenery with popa dear!' as if it was a cheap Sunday-school panorama! And what do these chuckle-headed women do but get off the coach and go to wanderin' about, and playin' 'here we go round the mulberry bush' until one of 'em tumbles down a ravine. And then there's a great to do! and 'dear popa' was up and down the road yellin' 'Me cheyld! me cheyld!' And then there was camphor and sal volatile and eau de cologne to be got, and the coach goes off, and 'popa dear' gets left, and then has to hurry off in a buggy to catch it. So *we* get left too, just because that God-forsaken fool, Neworth, brings his women here."

Under this recital poor Bray sat as completely crushed as when the fair daughter of Neworth had descended upon his shoulders at the spring. He saw it all! *His* was the fault. It was *his* delay and dalliance with her that had checked Neworth's visit; worse than that, it was his subsequent audacity and her defense of him that would probably prevent any renewal of the negotiations. He had shipwrecked his partners' prospects in his absurd vanity and pride! He did not dare to raise his eyes to their dejected faces. He would have confessed everything to them, but the same feeling of delicacy for her which had determined him to keep her adventures to himself now forever sealed his lips. How might they not misconstrue his conduct—and *hers*! Perhaps something of this was visible in his face.

"Come, old man," said the cheerful misogynist, with perfect innocence, "don't take it so hard. Some time in a man's life a woman's sure to get the drop on him, as I said afore, and this yer woman's got the drop on five of us! But—hallo, Ned, old man—what's the matter with your head?" He laid his hand gently on the matted temple of his younger partner.

"I had—a slip—on the trail," he stammered. "Had to go back again for another pailful. That's what delayed me, you know, boys," he added. "But it's nothing!"

"Nothing!" ejaculated Parkhurst, clapping him on the back and twisting him around by the shoulders so that he faced his companions. "Nothing! Look at him, gentlemen; and he says it's 'nothing.' That's how a *man* takes it! *He* didn't go round yellin' and wringin' his hands and sayin' 'Me pay-l! me pay-l!' when it spilt! He just humped himself and trotted back for another. And yet every drop of water in that overset bucket meant hard work and hard sweat, and was as precious as gold."

Luckily for Bray, whose mingled emotions under Parkhurst's eloquence were beginning to be hysterical, the foreman interrupted.

"Well, boys! it's time we got to work again, and took another heave at the old ledge! But now that this job of Neworth's is over—I don't mind tellin' ye suthin." As their leader usually spoke but little, and to the point, the four men gathered around him. "Although I engineered this affair, and got it up, somehow, I never *saw* that Neworth standing on this ledge! No, boys! I never saw him *here*." The look of superstition which Bray and the others had often seen on this old miner's face, and which so often showed itself in his acts, was there. "And though I wanted him to come, and allowed to have him come, I'm kinder relieved that he didn't, and so let whatsoever luck's in the air come to us five alone, boys, just as we stand."

The next morning Bray was up before his companions, and although it was not his turn, offered to bring water from the spring. He was not in love with Eugenia—he had not forgotten his remorse of the previous day—but he would like to go there once more before he relentlessly wiped out her image from his mind. And he had heard that although Neworth had gone on to Sacramento, his son and the two ladies had stopped on for a day or two at the ditch superintendent's house on the summit, only two miles away. She might pass on the road; he might get a glimpse of her again and a wave of her hand before this thing was over forever, and he should have to take up the daily routine of his work again. It was not love—of *that* he was assured—but it was the way to stop it by convincing himself of its madness. Besides, in view of all the circumstances, it was his duty as a gentleman to show some concern for her condition after the accident and the disagreeable contretemps which followed it.

Thus Bray! Alas, none of these possibilities occurred. He found the spring had simply lapsed into its
previous unsuggestive obscurity,—a mere niche in the
mountain side that held only—water! The stage road
was deserted save for an early, curly-headed schoolboy, whom he found lurking on the bank, but who
evaded his company and conversation. He returned
to the camp quite cured of his fancy. His late zeal
as a water-carrier had earned him a day or two's ex-
emption from that duty. His place was taken the next
afternoon by the woman-hating Parkhurst, and he
was the less concerned by it as he had heard that the
same afternoon the ladies were to leave the summit
for Sacramento.

But then occurred a singular coincidence. The new
water-bringer was as scandalously late in his delivery of
the precious fluid as his predecessor! An hour passed
and he did not return. His unfortunate partners, toiling away with pick and crowbar on the burning ledge,
were clamorous from thirst, and Bray was becoming
absurdly uneasy. It could not be possible that Eugenia's
accident had been repeated! Or had she met him with
inquiries? But no! she was already gone. The mystery
was presently cleared, however, by the abrupt appearance of Parkhurst running towards them, but *without
his pail*! The cry of consternation and despair which
greeted that discovery was, however, quickly changed
by a single breathless, half intelligible sentence he had
shot before him from his panting lips. And he was

holding something in his outstretched palm that was more eloquent than words. Gold!

In an instant they had him under the shade of the pine-tree, and were squatting round him like school-boys. He was profoundly agitated. His story, far from being brief, was incoherent and at times seemed irrelevant, but that was characteristic. They would remember that he had always held the theory that, even in quartz mining, the deposits were always found near water, past or present, with signs of fluvial erosion! He didn't call himself one of your blanked scientific miners, but his head was level! It was all very well for them to say "Yes, yes!" *now*, but they didn't use to! Well! when he got to the spring, he noticed that there had been a kind of landslide above it, of course, from water cleavage, and there was a distinct mark of it on the mountain side, where it had uprooted and thrown over some small bushes!

Excited as Bray was, he recognized with a hysterical sensation the track made by Eugenia in her fall, which he himself had noticed. But he had thought only of *her*.

"When I saw that," continued Parkhurst, more rapidly and coherently, "I saw that there was a crack above the hole where the water came through—as if it had been the old channel of the spring. I widened it a little with my clasp knife, and then—in a little pouch or pocket of decomposed quartz—I found that! Not only that, boys," he continued, rising, with a shout, "but the whole slope above the spring is a mass of seepage underneath, as if you'd played a hydraulic hose on it, and it's ready to tumble and is just rotten with quartz!"

The men leaped to their feet; in another moment they had snatched picks, pans, and shovels, and, the foreman leading, with a coil of rope thrown over his shoulders, were all flying down the trail to the highway. Their haste was wise. The spring was not on *their* claim; it was known to others; it was doubtful if Parkhurst's discovery with his knife amounted to actual *work* on the soil. They must "take it up" with a formal notice, and get to work at once!

In an hour they were scattered over the mountain side, like bees clinging to the fragrant slope of laurel and myrtle above the spring. An excavation was made beside it, and the ledge broadened by a dozen feet. Even the spring itself was utilized to wash the hastily filled prospecting pans. And when the Pioneer Coach slowly toiled up the road that afternoon, the passengers stared at the scarcely dry "Notice of Location" pinned to the pine by the road bank, whence Eugenia had fallen two days before!

Eagerly and anxiously as Edward Bray worked with his companions, it was with more conflicting feelings. There was a certain sense of desecration in their act. How her proud lip would have curled had she seen him—he who but a few hours before would have searched the whole slope for the treasure of a ribbon, a handkerchief, or a bow from her dress—now delving and picking the hillside for that fortune her accident had so mysteriously disclosed. Mysteriously he believed, for he had not fully accepted Parkhurst's story. That gentle misogynist had never been an active prospector; an inclination to theorize without practice and to combat his partners' experience were all against his alleged process of discovery, although the gold was actually there; and his conduct that afternoon was certainly peculiar. He did but little of the real work; but wandered from man to man, with suggestions, advice, and exhortations, and the air of a superior patron. This might have been characteristic, but mingled with it was a certain nervous anxiety and watchfulness. He was continually scanning the stage road and the trail, staring eagerly at any wayfarer in the distance, and at times falling into fits of strange abstraction. At other times he would draw near to one of his fellow partners, as if for confidential disclosure, and then check himself and wander aimlessly away. And it was not until evening came that the mystery was solved.

The prospecting pans had been duly washed and examined, the slope above and below had been fully explored and tested, with a result and promise that outran their most sanguine hopes. There was no mistaking the fact that they had made a "big" strike. That singular gravity and reticence, so often observed in miners at these crises, had come over them as they sat that night for the last time around their old camp-fire on the Eureka ledge, when Parkhurst turned impulsively to Bray. "Roll over here," he said in a whisper. "I want to tell ye suthin!"

Bray "rolled" beyond the squatting circle, and the two men gradually edged themselves out of hearing of the others. In the silent abstraction that prevailed nobody noticed them.

"It's got suthin to do with this discovery," said Parkhurst, in a low, mysterious tone, "but as far as the gold goes, and our equal rights to it as partners, it don't affect them. If I," he continued in a slightly patronizing, paternal tone, "choose to make you and the other boys sharers in what seems to be a special Providence to *me*, I reckon we won't quarrel on it. It's a mighty curious, singular thing. It's one of those things ye read about in books and don't take any stock in! But we've got the gold—and I've got the black and white to prove it—even if it ain't exactly human."

His voice sank so low, his manner was so impressive, that despite his known exaggeration, Bray felt a slight thrill of superstition. Meantime Parkhurst wiped his brow, took a folded slip of paper and a sprig of laurel from his pocket, and drew a long breath.

"When I got to the spring this afternoon," he went on, in a nervous, tremulous, and scarcely audible voice, "I saw this bit o' paper, folded note-wise, lyin' on the ledge before it. On top of it was this sprig of laurel, to catch the eye. I ain't the man to pry into other folks' secrets, or read what ain't mine. But on the back o' this note was written 'To Jack!' It's a common enough name, but it's a singular thing, ef you'll recollect, thar ain't *another* Jack in this company, not on the whole ridge betwixt this and the summit, except *myself*! So

I opened it, and this is what it read!" He held the paper sideways toward the leaping light of the still near camp-fire, and read slowly, with the emphasis of having read it many times before.

"'I want you to believe that I, at least, respect and honor your honest, manly calling, and when you strike it rich, as you surely will, I hope you will sometimes think of Jill.'"

In the thrill of joy, hope, and fear that came over Bray, he could see that Parkhurst had not only failed to detect his secret, but had not even connected the two names with their obvious suggestion. "But do you know anybody named Jill?" he asked breathlessly.

"It's no *name*," said Parkhurst in a sombre voice, "it's a *thing*!"

"A thing?" repeated Bray, bewildered.

"Yes, a measure—you know—two fingers of whiskey."

"Oh, a 'gill,'" said Bray.

"That's what I said, young man," returned Parkhurst gravely.

Bray choked back a hysterical laugh; spelling was notoriously not one of Parkhurst's strong points. "But what has a 'gill' got to do with it?" he asked quickly.

"It's one of them Sphinx things, don't you see? A sort of riddle or rebus, you know. You've got to study it out, as them old chaps did. But I fetched it. What comes after 'gills,' eh?"

"Pints, I suppose," said Bray.

"And after pints?"

"Quarts."

"*Quartz*, and there you are. So I looked about me for quartz, and sure enough struck it the first pop."

Bray cast a quick look at Parkhurst's grave face. The man was evidently impressed and sincere. "Have you told this to any one?" he asked quickly.

"No."

"Then *don't*! or you'll spoil the charm, and bring us ill luck! That's the rule, you know. I really don't know that you ought to have told me," added the artful Bray, dissembling his intense joy at this proof of Eugenia's remembrance.

"But," said Parkhurst blankly, "you see, old man, you'd been the last man at the spring, and I kinder thought"—

"Don't think," said Bray promptly, "and above all, don't talk; not a word to the boys of this. Stay! Give me the paper and the sprig. I've got to go to San Francisco next week, and I'll take care of it and think it out!" He knew that Parkhurst might be tempted to talk, but without the paper his story would be treated lightly. Parkhurst handed him the paper, and the two men returned to the camp-fire.

That night Bray slept but little. The superstition of the lover is no less keen than that of the gambler, and Bray, while laughing at Parkhurst's extravagant fancy, I am afraid was equally inclined to believe that their good fortune came through Eugenia's influence. At least he should tell her so, and her precious note became now an invitation as well as an excuse for seeking her. The only fear that possessed him was that she might have expected some acknowledgment of her note before she left that afternoon; the only thing he could not understand was how she had managed to convey the note to the spring, for she could not have taken it herself. But this would doubtless be explained by her in San Francisco, whither he intended to seek her. His affairs, the purchasing of machinery for their new claim, would no doubt give him easy access to her father.

But it was one thing to imagine this while procuring a new and fashionable outfit in San Francisco, and quite another to stand before the "palatial" residence of the Neworths on Rincon Hill, with the consciousness of no other introduction than the memory of the Neworths' discourtesy on the mountain, and, even in his fine feathers, Bray hesitated. At this moment a carriage rolled up to the door, and Eugenia, an adorable vision of laces and silks, alighted.

Forgetting everything else, he advanced toward her with outstretched hand. He saw her start, a faint color come into her face; he knew he was recognized; but she stiffened quickly again, the color vanished, her beautiful gray eyes rested coldly on him for a moment, and then, with the faintest inclination of her proud head, she swept by him and entered the house.

But Bray, though shocked, was not daunted, and perhaps his own pride was awakened. He ran to his hotel, summoned a messenger, inclosed her note in an envelope, and added these lines:—

Dear Miss Neworth,

I only wanted to thank you an hour ago, as I should like to have done before, for the kind note which I inclose, but which you have made me feel I have no right to treasure any longer, and to tell you that your most generous wish and prophecy has been more than fulfilled.

Yours, very gratefully,
Edmund Bray.

Within the hour the messenger returned with the still briefer reply:—

"Miss Neworth has been fully aware of that preoccupation with his good fortune which prevented Mr. Bray from an earlier acknowledgment of her foolish note."

Cold as this response was, Bray's heart leaped. She *had* lingered on the summit, and *had* expected a reply. He seized his hat, and, jumping into the first cab at the hotel door, drove rapidly back to the house. He had but one idea, to see her at any cost, but one concern, to avoid a meeting with her father first, or a denial at her very door.

He dismissed the cab at the street corner and began to reconnoitre the house. It had a large garden in the rear, reclaimed from the adjacent "scrub oak" infested sand hill, and protected by a high wall. If he could scale that wall, he could command the premises. It was a bright morning; she might be tempted into the garden. A taller scrub oak grew near the wall; to the mountain-bred Bray it was an easy matter to swing himself from it to the wall, and he did. But his momentum was so great that he touched the wall only to be obliged to leap down into the garden to save himself from falling there. He heard a little cry, felt his feet strike some tin utensil, and rolled on the ground beside Eugenia and her overturned watering-pot.

They both struggled to their feet with an astonishment that turned to laughter in their eyes and the same thought in the minds of each.

"But we are not on the mountains now, Mr. Bray," said Eugenia, taking her handkerchief at last from her sobering face and straightening eyebrows.

"But we are quits," said Bray. "And you now know my real name. I only came here to tell you why I could not answer your letter the same day. I never got it—I mean," he added hurriedly, "another man got it first."

She threw up her head, and her face grew pale. "*Another* man got it," she repeated, "and *you* let another man"—

"No, no," interrupted Bray imploringly. "You don't understand. One of my partners went to the spring that afternoon, and found it; but he neither knows who sent it, nor for whom it was intended." He hastily recounted Parkhurst's story, his mysterious belief, and his interpretation of the note. The color came back to her face and the smile to her lips and eyes. "I had gone twice to the spring after I saw you, but I couldn't bear its deserted look without you," he added boldly. Here, seeing her face grew grave again, he added, "But how did you get the letter to the spring? and how did you know that it was found that day?"

It was her turn to look embarrassed and entreating, but the combination was charming in her proud face. "I got the little schoolboy at the summit," she said, with girlish hesitation, "to take the note. He knew the spring, but he didn't know *you*. I told him— it was very foolish, I know—to wait until you came for water, to be certain that you got the note, to wait until you came up, for I thought you might question him, or give him some word." Her face was quite rosy now. "But," she added, and her lip took a divine pout, "he said he waited *two hours*; that you never took the *least concern* of the letter or him, but went around the mountain side, peering and picking in every hole and corner of it, and then he got tired and ran away. Of course I understand it now, it wasn't *you*; but oh, please; I beg you, Mr. Bray, don't!"

Bray released the little hand which he had impulsively caught, and which had allowed itself to be detained for a blissful moment.

"And now, don't you think, Mr. Bray," she added demurely, "that you had better let me fill my pail again while you go round to the front door and call upon me properly?"

"But your father"—

"My father, as a well-known investor, regrets exceedingly that he did not make your acquaintance more thoroughly in his late brief interview. He is, as your foreman knows, exceedingly interested in the mines on Eureka ledge. He will be glad if you will call." She led him to a little door in the wall, which she unbolted. "And now 'Jill' must say good-by to 'Jack,' for she must make herself ready to receive a Mr. Bray who is expected."

And when Bray a little later called at the front door, he was respectfully announced. He called another day, and many days after. He came frequently to San Francisco, and one day did not return to his old partners. He had entered into a new partnership with one who he declared "had made the first strike on Eureka mountain."

Mr. Bilson's Housekeeper

I

When Joshua Bilson, of the Summit House, Buckeye Hill, lost his wife, it became necessary for him to take a housekeeper to assist him in the management of the hotel. Already all Buckeye had considered this a mere preliminary to taking another wife, after a decent probation, as the relations of housekeeper and landlord were confidential and delicate, and Bilson was a man, and not above female influence. There was, however, some change of opinion on that point when Miss Euphemia Trotter was engaged for that position. Buckeye Hill, which had confidently looked forward to a buxom widow or, with equal confidence, to the promotion of some pretty but inefficient chambermaid, was startled by the selection of a maiden lady of middle age, and above the medium height, at once serious, precise, and masterful, and to all appearances outrageously competent. More carefully "taking stock" of her, it was accepted she had three good points,— dark, serious eyes, a trim but somewhat thin figure, and well-kept hands and feet. These, which in so susceptible a community would have been enough, in the words of one critic, "to have married her to three men," she seemed to make of little account herself, and her attitude toward those who were inclined to make them of account was ceremonious and frigid. Indeed, she seemed to occupy herself entirely with looking after the servants, Chinese and Europeans, examining the bills and stores of traders and shopkeepers, in a fashion that made her respected and—feared. It was whispered, in fact, that Bilson stood in awe of her as he never had of his wife, and that he was "henpecked in his own farmyard by a strange pullet."

Nevertheless, he always spoke of her with a respect and even a reverence that seemed incompatible with their relative positions. It gave rise to surmises more or less ingenious and conflicting: Miss Trotter had a secret interest in the hotel, and represented a San Francisco syndicate; Miss Trotter was a woman of independent property, and had advanced large sums to Bilson; Miss Trotter was a woman of no property, but she was the only daughter of—variously—a late distinguished nobleman, a ruined millionaire, and a foreign statesman, bent on making her own living.

Alas, for romance! Miss Euphemia Trotter, or "Miss E. Trotter," as she preferred to sign herself, loathing her sentimental prefix, was really a poor girl who had been educated in an Eastern seminary, where she eventually became a teacher. She had survived her parents and a neglected childhood, and had worked hard for her living since she was fourteen. She had been a nurse in a hospital, an assistant in a reformatory, had observed men and women under conditions of pain and weakness, and had known the body only as a tabernacle of helplessness and suffering; yet had brought out of her experience a hard philosophy which she used equally to herself as to others. That she had ever indulged in any romance of human existence, I greatly doubt; the lanky girl teacher at the Vermont academy had enough to do to push herself forward without entangling girl friendships or confidences, and so became a prematurely hard duenna, paid to look out for, restrain, and report, if necessary, any vagrant flirtation or small intrigue of her companions. A pronounced "old maid" at fifteen, she had nothing to forget or forgive in others, and still less to learn from them.

It was spring, and down the long slopes of Buckeye Hill the flowers were already effacing the last dented footprints of the winter rains, and the winds no longer brought their monotonous patter. In the pine woods there were the song and flash of birds, and the quickening stimulus of the stirring aromatic sap. Miners and tunnelmen were already forsaking the direct road for a ramble through the woodland trail and its sylvan charms, and occasionally breaking into shouts and horseplay like great boys. The schoolchildren were disporting there; there were some older couples sentimentally gathering flowers side by side. Miss Trotter was also there, but making a short cut from the bank and express office, and by no means disturbed by any gentle reminiscence of her girlhood or any other instinctive participation in the wanton season. Spring came, she knew, regularly every year, and brought "spring cleaning" and other necessary changes and re-habilitations. This year it had brought also a consider-able increase in the sum she was putting by, and she was, perhaps, satisfied in a practical way, if not with the blind instinctiveness of others. She was walking leisurely, holding her gray skirt well over her slim an-kles and smartly booted feet, and clear of the brushing of daisies and buttercups, when suddenly she stopped. A few paces before her, partly concealed by a myrtle, a young woman, startled at her approach, had just with-drawn herself from the embrace of a young man and slipped into the shadow. Nevertheless, in that mo-ment, Miss Trotter's keen eyes had recognized her as a very pretty Swedish girl, one of her chambermaids at the hotel. Miss Trotter passed without a word, but gravely. She was not shocked nor surprised, but it struck her practical mind at once that if this were an affair with impending matrimony, it meant the loss of a valuable and attractive servant; if otherwise, a seri-ous disturbance of that servant's duties. She must look out for another girl to take the place of Frida Pauline Jansen, that was all. It is possible, therefore, that Miss Jansen's criticism of Miss Trotter to her companion as a "spying, jealous old cat" was unfair. This com-panion Miss Trotter had noticed, only to observe that his face and figure were unfamiliar to her. His red shirt and heavy boots gave no indication of his social condition in that locality. He seemed more startled and disturbed at her intrusion than the girl had been, but that was more a condition of sex than of degree, she also knew. In such circumstances it is the woman always who is the most composed and self-possessed.

A few days after this, Miss Trotter was summoned in some haste to the office. Chris Calton, a young man of twenty-six, partner in the Roanoke Ledge, had fractured his arm and collar-bone by a fall, and had been brought to the hotel for that rest and attention, under medical advice, which he could not procure in the Roanoke company's cabin. She had a retired, quiet room made ready. When he was installed there by the doctor she went to see him, and found a good-looking, curly headed young fellow, even boyish in appearance and manner, who received her with that air of deference and timidity which she was accustomed to excite in the masculine breast—when it was not accompanied with distrust. It struck her that he was somewhat emotional, and had the expression of one who had been spoiled and petted by women, a rather unusual circumstance among the men of the locality. Perhaps it would be unfair to her to say that a disposition to show him that he could expect no such "nonsense" *there* sprang up in her heart at that moment, for she never had understood any tolerance of such weakness, but a certain precision and dryness of manner was the only result of her observation. She adjusted his pillow, asked him if there was anything that he wanted, but took her directions from the doctor, rather than from himself, with a practical insight and minuteness that was as appalling to the patient as it was an unexpected delight to Dr. Duchesne. "I see you quite understand me, Miss Trotter," he said, with great relief.

"I ought to," responded the lady dryly. "I had a dozen such cases, some of them with complications, while I was assistant at the Sacramento Hospital."

"Ah, then!" returned the doctor, dropping gladly into purely professional detail, "you'll see this is very simple, not a comminuted fracture; constitution and blood healthy; all you've to do is to see that he eats properly, keeps free from excitement and worry, but does not get despondent; a little company; his partners and some of the boys from the Ledge will drop in occasionally; not too much of *them*, you know; and of course, absolute immobility of the injured parts." The lady nodded; the patient lifted his blue eyes for an instant to hers with a look of tentative appeal, but it slipped off Miss Trotter's dark pupils—which were as abstractedly critical as the doctor's—without being absorbed by them. When the door closed behind her, the doctor exclaimed: "By Jove! you're in luck, Chris! That's a splendid woman! Just the one to look after you!" The patient groaned slightly. "Do what she says, and we'll pull you through in no time. Why! she's able to adjust those bandages herself!"

This, indeed, she did a week later, when the surgeon had failed to call, unveiling his neck and arm with professional coolness, and supporting him in her slim arms against her stiff, erect buckramed breast, while she replaced the splints with masculine firmness of touch and serene and sexless indifference. His stammered embarrassed thanks at the relief—for he had been in considerable pain—she accepted with a certain pride as a tribute to her skill, a tribute which Dr. Duchesne himself afterward fully indorsed.

On re-entering his room the third or fourth morning after his advent at the Summit House, she noticed with some concern that there was a slight flush on his cheek and a certain exaltation which she at first thought presaged fever. But an examination of his pulse and temperature dispelled that fear, and his talkativeness and good spirits convinced her that it was only his youthful vigor at last overcoming his despondency. A few days later, this cheerfulness not being continued, Dr. Duchesne followed Miss Trotter into the hall. "We must try to keep our patient from moping in his confinement, you know," he began, with a slight smile, "and he seems to be somewhat of an emotional nature, accustomed to be amused and—er—er—petted."

"His friends were here yesterday," returned Miss Trotter dryly, "but I did not interfere with them until I thought they had stayed long enough to suit your wishes."

"I am not referring to *them*," said the doctor, still smiling; "but you know a woman's sympathy and presence in a sickroom is often the best of tonics or sedatives."

Miss Trotter raised her eyes to the speaker with a half critical impatience.

"The fact is," the doctor went on, "I have a favor to ask of you for our patient. It seems that the other morning a new chambermaid waited upon him, whom he found much more gentle and sympathetic in her manner than the others, and more submissive and quiet in her ways—possibly because she is a foreigner, and accustomed to servitude. I suppose you have no objection to *her* taking charge of his room?"

Miss Trotter's cheek slightly flushed. Not from wounded vanity, but from the consciousness of some want of acumen that had made her make a mistake. She had really believed, from her knowledge of the patient's character and the doctor's preamble, that he wished *her* to show some more kindness and personal sympathy to the young man, and had even been prepared to question its utility! She saw her blunder quickly, and at once remembering that the pretty Swedish girl had one morning taken the place of an absent fellow servant, in the rebound from her error, she said quietly: "You mean Frida! Certainly! she can look after his room, if he prefers her." But for her blunder she might have added conscientiously that she thought the girl would prove inefficient, but she did not. She remembered the incident of the wood; yet if the girl had a lover in the wood, she could not urge it as a proof of incapacity. She gave the necessary orders, and the incident passed.

Visiting the patient a few days afterward, she could not help noticing a certain shy gratitude in Mr. Calton's greeting of her, which she quietly ignored.

This forced the ingenuous Chris to more positive speech. He dwelt with great simplicity and enthusiasm on the Swedish girl's gentleness and sympathy. "You have no idea of—her—natural tenderness, Miss Trotter," he stammered naively. Miss Trotter, remembering the wood, thought to herself that she had some faint idea of it, but did not impart what it was. He spoke also of her beauty, not being clever enough to affect an indifference or ignorance of it, which made Miss Trotter respect him and smile an unqualified acquiescence. Frida certainly was pretty! But when he spoke of her as "Miss Jansen," and said she was so much more "ladylike and refined than the other servants," she replied by asking him if his bandages hurt him, and, receiving a negative answer, graciously withdrew.

Indeed, his bandages gave him little trouble now, and his improvement was so marked and sustained that the doctor was greatly gratified, and, indeed, expressed as much to Miss Trotter, with the conscientious addition that he believed the greater part of it was due to her capable nursing! "Yes, ma'am, he has to thank *you* for it, and no one else!"

Miss Trotter raised her dark eyes and looked steadily at him. Accustomed as he was to men and women, the look strongly held him. He saw in her eyes an intelligence equal to his own, a knowledge of good and evil, and a toleration and philosophy, equal to his own, but a something else that was as distinct and different as their sex. And therein lay its charm, for it merely translated itself in his mind that she had very pretty eyes, which he had never noticed before, without any aggressive intellectual quality. And with this, alas! came the man's propensity to reason. It meant of course but *one* thing; he saw it all now! If *he*, in his preoccupation and coolness, had noticed her eyes, so also had the younger and emotional Chris. The young fellow was in love with her! It was that which had stimulated his recovery, and she was wondering if he, the doctor, had observed it. He smiled back the superior smile of our sex in moments of great inanity, and poor Miss Trotter believed he understood her. A few days after this, she noticed that Frida Jansen was wearing a pearl ring and a somewhat ostentatious locket. She remembered now that Mr. Bilson had told her that the Roanoke Ledge was very rich, and that Calton was likely to prove a profitable guest. But it was not *her* business.

It became her business, however, some days later, when Mr. Calton was so much better that he could sit in a chair, or even lounge listlessly in the hall and corridor. It so chanced that she was passing along the upper hall when she saw Frida's pink cotton skirt disappear in an adjacent room, and heard her light laugh as the door closed. But the room happened to be a card-room reserved exclusively for gentlemen's poker or euchre parties, and the chambermaids had no business there. Miss Trotter had no doubt that Mr. Calton was there, and that Frida knew it; but as this was an indiscretion so open, flagrant, and likely to be discovered by the first passing guest, she called to her sharply. She was astonished, however, at the same moment to see Mr. Calton walking in the corridor at some distance from the room in question. Indeed, she was so confounded that when Frida appeared from the room a little flurried, but with a certain audacity new to her, Miss Trotter withheld her rebuke, and sent her off on an imaginary errand, while she herself opened the card-room door. It contained simply Mr. Bilson, her employer; his explanation was glaringly embarrassed and unreal! Miss Trotter affected obliviousness, but was silent; perhaps she thought her employer was better able to take care of himself than Mr. Calton.

A week later this tension terminated by the return of Calton to Roanoke Ledge, a convalescent man. A very pretty watch and chain afterward were received by Miss Trotter, with a few lines expressing the gratitude of the ex-patient. Mr. Bilson was highly delighted, and frequently borrowed the watch to show to his guests as an advertisement of the healing powers of the Summit Hotel. What Mr. Calton sent to the more attractive and flirtatious Frida did not as publicly appear, and possibly Mr. Bilson did not know it. The incident of the cardroom was forgotten. Since that discovery, Miss Trotter had felt herself debarred from taking the girl's conduct into serious account, and it did not interfere with her work.

II

One afternoon Miss Trotter received a message that Mr. Calton desired a few moments' private conversation with her. A little curious, she had him shown into one of the sitting-rooms, but was surprised on entering to find that she was in the presence of an utter stranger! This was explained by the visitor saying briefly that he was Chris's elder brother, and that he presumed the name would be sufficient introduction. Miss Trotter smiled doubtfully, for a more distinct opposite to Chris could not be conceived. The stranger was apparently strong, practical, and masterful in all those qualities in which his brother was charmingly weak. Miss Trotter, for no reason whatever, felt herself inclined to resent them.

"I reckon, Miss Trotter," he said bluntly, "that you don't know anything of this business that brings me here. At least," he hesitated, with a certain rough courtesy, "I should judge from your general style and gait that you wouldn't have let it go on so far if you had, but the fact is, that darned fool brother of mine— beg your pardon!—has gone and got himself engaged to one of the girls that help here,—a yellow-haired foreigner, called Frida Jansen."

"I was not aware that it had gone so far as that," said Miss Trotter quietly, "although his admiration for her was well known, especially to his doctor, at whose request I selected her to especially attend to your brother."

"The doctor is a fool," broke in Mr. Calton abruptly. "He only thought of keeping Chris quiet while he finished his job."

"And really, Mr. Calton," continued Miss Trotter, ignoring the interruption, "I do not see what right I have to interfere with the matrimonial intentions of any guest in this house, even though or—as you seem to put it—*because* the object of his attentions is in its employ."

Mr. Calton stared—angrily at first, and then with a kind of wondering amazement that any woman—above all a housekeeper—should take such a view. "But," he stammered, "I thought you—you—looked after the conduct of those girls."

"I'm afraid you've assumed too much," said Miss Trotter placidly. "My business is to see that they attend to their duties here. Frida Jansen's duty was—as I have just told you—to look after your brother's room. And as far as I understand you, you are not here to complain of her inattention to that duty, but of its resulting in an attachment on your brother's part, and, as you tell me, an intention as to her future, which is really the one thing that would make my 'looking after her conduct' an impertinence and interference! If you had come to tell me that he did *not* intend to marry her, but was hurting her reputation, I could have understood and respected your motives."

Mr. Calton felt his face grow red and himself discomfited. He had come there with the firm belief that he would convict Miss Trotter of a grave fault, and that in her penitence she would be glad to assist him in breaking off the match. On the contrary, to find himself arraigned and put on his defense by this tall, slim woman, erect and smartly buckramed in logic and whalebone, was preposterous! But it had the effect of subduing his tone.

"You don't understand," he said awkwardly yet pleadingly. "My brother is a fool, and any woman could wind him round her finger. *She* knows it. She knows he is rich and a partner in the Roanoke Ledge. That's all she wants. She is not a fit match for him. I've said he was a fool—but, hang it all! that's no reason why he should marry an ignorant girl—a foreigner and a servant—when he could do better elsewhere."

"This would seem to be a matter between you and your brother, and not between myself and my servant," said Miss Trotter coldly. "If you cannot convince *him*, your own brother, I do not see how you expect me to convince *her*, a servant, over whom I have no control except as a mistress of her *work*, when, on your own showing, she has everything to gain by the marriage. If you wish Mr. Bilson, the proprietor, to threaten her with dismissal unless she gives up your brother,"— Miss Trotter smiled inwardly at the thought of the card-room incident,—"it seems to me you might only precipitate the marriage."

Mr. Calton looked utterly blank and hopeless. His reason told him that she was right. More than that, a certain admiration for her clear-sightedness began to possess him, with the feeling that he would like to have "shown up" a little better than he had in this interview. If Chris had fallen in love with *her*—but Chris was a fool and wouldn't have appreciated her!

"But you might talk with her, Miss Trotter," he said, now completely subdued. "Even if you could not reason her out of it, you might find out what she expects from this marriage. If you would talk to her as sensibly as you have to me"—

"It is not likely that she will seek my assistance as you have," said Miss Trotter, with a faint smile which Mr. Calton thought quite pretty, "but I will see about it."

Whatever Miss Trotter intended to do did not transpire. She certainly was in no hurry about it, as she did not say anything to Frida that day, and the next afternoon it so chanced that business took her to the bank and post-office. Her way home again lay through the Summit woods. It recalled to her the memorable occasion when she was first a witness to Frida's flirtations. Neither that nor Mr. Bilson's presumed gallantries, however, seemed inconsistent, in Miss Trotter's knowledge of the world, with a serious engagement with young Calton. She was neither shocked nor horrified by it, and for that reason she had not thought it necessary to speak of it to the elder Mr. Calton.

Her path wound through a thicket fragrant with syringa and southernwood; the faint perfume was reminiscent of Atlantic hillsides, where, long ago, a girl teacher, she had walked with the girl pupils of the Vermont academy, and kept them from the shy advances of the local swains. She smiled—a little sadly—as the thought occurred to her that after this interval of years it was again her business to restrain the callow affections. Should she never have the matchmaking instincts of her sex; never become the trusted confidante of youthful passion? Young Calton had not confessed his passion to *her*, nor had Frida revealed her secret. Only the elder brother had appealed to her hard, practical common sense against such sentiment. Was there something in her manner that forbade it? She wondered if it was some uneasy consciousness of this quality which had impelled her to snub the elder Calton, and rebelled against it.

It was quite warm; she had been walking a little faster than her usual deliberate gait, and checked herself, halting in the warm breath of the syringas. Here she heard her name called in a voice that she recognized, but in tones so faint and subdued that it seemed to her part of her thoughts. She turned quickly and beheld Chris Calton a few feet from her, panting, partly from running and partly from some nervous embarrassment. His handsome but weak mouth was expanded in an apologetic smile; his blue eyes shone with a kind of youthful appeal so inconsistent with his long brown mustache and broad shoulders that she was divided between a laugh and serious concern.

"I saw you—go into the wood—but I lost you," he said, breathing quickly, "and then when I did see you again—you were walking so fast I had to run after you. I wanted—to speak—to you—if you'll let me. I won't detain you—I can walk your way."

Miss Trotter was a little softened, but not so much as to help him out with his explanation. She drew her neat skirts aside, and made way for him on the path beside her.

"You see," he went on nervously, taking long strides to her shorter ones, and occasionally changing sides in his embarrassment, "my brother Jim has been talking to you about my engagement to Frida, and trying to put you against her and me. He said as much to me, and added you half promised to help him! But I didn't believe him—Miss Trotter!—I know you wouldn't do it—you haven't got it in your heart to hurt a poor girl! He says he has every confidence in you—that you're worth a dozen such girls as she is, and that I'm a big fool or I'd see it. I don't say you're not all he says, Miss Trotter; but I'm not such a fool as he thinks, for I know your *goodness* too. I know how you tended me when I was ill, and how you sent Frida to comfort me. You know, too,—for you're a woman yourself,—that all you could say, or anybody could, wouldn't separate two people who loved each other."

Miss Trotter for the first time felt embarrassed, and this made her a little angry. "I don't think I gave your brother any right to speak for me or of me in this matter," she said icily; "and if you are quite satisfied, as you say you are, of your own affection and Frida's, I do not see why you should care for anybody'sinterference."

"Now you are angry with me," he said in a doleful voice which at any other time would have excited her mirth; "and I've just done it. Oh, Miss Trotter, don't! Please forgive me! I didn't mean to say your talk was no good. I didn't mean to say you couldn't help us. Please don't be mad at me!"

He reached out his hand, grasped her slim fingers in his own, and pressed them, holding them and even arresting her passage. The act was without familiarity or boldness, and she felt that to snatch her hand away would be an imputation of that meaning, instead of the boyish impulse that prompted it. She gently withdrew her hand as if to continue her walk, and said, with a smile:—

"Then you confess you need help—in what way?"

"With her!"

Miss Trotter stared. "With *her*!" she repeated. This was a new idea. Was it possible that this common, ignorant girl was playing and trifling with her golden opportunity? "Then you are not quite sure of her?" she said a little coldly.

"She's so high spirited, you know," he said humbly, "and so attractive, and if she thought my friends objected and were saying unkind things of her,—well!"—he threw out his hands with a suggestion of hopeless despair—"there's no knowing what she might do."

Miss Trotter's obvious thought was that Frida knew on which side her bread was buttered; but remembering that the proprietor was a widower, it occurred to her that the young woman might also have it buttered on both sides. Her momentary fancy of uniting two lovers somehow weakened at this suggestion, and there was a hardening of her face as she said, "Well, if *you* can't trust her, perhaps your brother may be right."

"I don't say that, Miss Trotter," said Chris pleadingly, yet with a slight wincing at her words; "*you* could convince her, if you would only try. Only let her see that she has some other friends beside myself. Look! Miss Trotter, I'll leave it all to you—there! If you will only help me, I will promise not to see her— not to go near her again—until you have talked with her. There! Even my brother would not object to that. And if he has every confidence in you, I'm showing you I've more—don't you see? Come, now, promise— won't you, dear Miss Trotter?" He again took her hand, and this time pressed a kiss upon her slim fingers. And this time she did not withdraw them. Indeed, it seemed to her, in the quick recurrence of her previous sympathy, as if a hand had been put into her loveless past, grasping and seeking hers in its loneliness. None of her school friends had ever appealed to her like this simple, weak, and loving young man. Perhaps it was because they were of her own sex, and she distrusted them.

Nevertheless, this momentary weakness did not disturb her good common sense. She looked at him fixedly for a moment, and then said, with a faint smile, "Perhaps she does not trust *you*. Perhaps you cannot trust yourself."

He felt himself reddening with a strange embarrassment. It was not so much the question that disturbed him as the eyes of Miss Trotter; eyes that he had never before noticed as being so beautiful in their color, clearness, and half tender insight. He dropped her hand with a new-found timidity, and yet with a feeling that he would like to hold it longer.

"I mean," she said, stopping short in the trail at a point where a fringe of almost impenetrable "buckeyes" marked the extreme edge of the woods,—"I mean that you are still very young, and as Frida is nearly your own age,"—she could not resist this peculiarly feminine innuendo,—"she may doubt your ability to marry her in the face of opposition; she may even think my interference is a proof of it; but," she added quickly, to relieve his embarrassment and a certain abstracted look with which he was beginning to regard her, "I will speak to her, and," she concluded playfully, "you must take the consequences."

He said "Thank you," but not so earnestly as his previous appeal might have suggested, and with the same awkward abstraction in his eyes. Miss Trotter did not notice it, as her own eyes were at that moment fixed upon a point on the trail a few rods away. "Look," she said in a lower voice, "I may have the opportunity now for there is Frida herself passing." Chris turned in the direction of her glance. It was indeed the young girl walking leisurely ahead of them. There was no mistaking the smart pink calico gown in which Frida was wont to array her rather generous figure, nor the long yellow braids that hung Marguerite-wise down her back. With the consciousness of good looks which she always carried, there was, in spite of her affected ease, a slight furtiveness in the occasional swift turn of her head, as if evading or seeking observation.

"I will overtake her and speak to her now," continued Miss Trotter. "I may not have so good a chance again to see her alone. You can wait here for my return, if you like."

Chris started out of his abstraction. "Stay!" he stammered, with a faint, tentative smile. "Perhaps— don't you think?—I had better go first and tell her you want to see her. I can send her here. You see, she might"—He stopped.

Miss Trotter smiled. "It was part of your promise, you know, that you were *not* to see her again until I had spoken. But no matter! Have it as you wish. I will wait here. Only be quick. She has just gone into the grove."

Without another word the young man turned away, and she presently saw him walking toward the pine grove into which Frida had disappeared. Then she cleared a space among the matted moss and chickweed, and, gathering her skirts about her, sat down to wait. The unwonted attitude, the whole situation, and the part that she seemed destined to take in this sentimental comedy affected her like some quaint child's play out of her lost youth, and she smiled, albeit with a little heightening of color and lively brightening of her eyes. Indeed, as she sat there listlessly probing the roots of the mosses with the point of her parasol, the casual passer-by might have taken herself for the heroine of some love tryst. She had a faint consciousness of this as she glanced to the right and left, wondering what any one from the hotel who saw her would think of her sylvan rendezvous; and as the recollection of Chris kissing her hand suddenly came back to her, her smile became a nervous laugh, and she found herself actually blushing!

But she was recalled to herself as suddenly. Chris was returning. He was walking directly towards her with slow, determined steps, quite different from his previous nervous agitation, and as he drew nearer she saw with some concern an equally strange change in his appearance: his colorful face was pale, his eyes fixed, and he looked ten years older. She rose quickly.

"I came back to tell you," he said, in a voice from which all trace of his former agitation had passed, "that I relieve you of your promise. It won't be necessary for you to see—Frida. I thank you all the same, Miss Trotter," he said, avoiding her eyes with a slight return to his boyish manner. "It was kind of you to promise to undertake a foolish errand for me, and to wait here, and the best thing I can do is to take myself off now and keep you no longer. Please don't ask me *why*. Sometime I may tell you, but not now."

"Then you have seen her?" asked Miss Trotter quickly, premising Frida's refusal from his face.

He hesitated a moment, then he said gravely, "Yes. Don't ask me any more, Miss Trotter, please.

Good-by!" He paused, and then, with a slight, uneasy glance toward the pine grove, "Don't let me keep you waiting here any longer." He took her hand, held it lightly for a moment, and said, "Go, now."

Miss Trotter, slightly bewildered and unsatisfied, nevertheless passed obediently out into the trail. He gazed after her for a moment, and then turned and began rapidly to ascend the slope where he had first overtaken her, and was soon out of sight. Miss Trotter continued her way home; but when she had reached the confines of the wood she turned, as if taking some sudden resolution, and began slowly to retrace her steps in the direction of the pine grove. What she expected to see there, possibly she could not have explained; what she actually saw after a moment's waiting were the figures of Frida and Mr. Bilson issuing from the shade! Her respected employer wore an air of somewhat ostentatious importance mingled with rustic gallantry. Frida's manner was also conscious with gratified vanity; and although they believed themselves alone, her voice was already pitched into a high key of nervous affectation, indicative of the peasant. But there was nothing to suggest that Chris had disturbed them in their privacy and confidences. Yet he had evidently seen enough to satisfy himself of her faithlessness. Had he ever suspected it before?

Miss Trotter waited only until they had well preceded her, and then took a shorter cut home. She was quite prepared that evening for an interview which Mr. Bilson requested. She found him awkward and embarrassed in her cool, self-possessed presence. He said he deemed it his duty to inform her of his approaching marriage with Miss Jansen; but it was because he wished distinctly to assure her that it would make no difference in Miss Trotter's position in the hotel, except to promote her to the entire control of the establishment. He was to be married in San Francisco at once, and he and his wife were to go abroad for a year or two; indeed, he contemplated eventually retiring from business. If Mr. Bilson was uneasily conscious during this interview that he had once paid attentions to Miss Trotter, which she had ignored, she never betrayed the least recollection of it. She thanked him for his confidence and wished him happiness.

Sudden as was this good fortune to Miss Trotter, an independence she had so often deservedly looked forward to, she was, nevertheless, keenly alive to the fact that she had attained it partly through Chris's disappointment and unhappiness. Her sane mind taught her that it was better for him; that he had been saved an ill-assorted marriage; that the girl had virtually rejected him for Bilson before he had asked her mediation that morning. Yet these reasons failed to satisfy her feelings. It seemed cruel to her that the interest which she had suddenly taken in poor Chris should end so ironically in disaster to her sentiment and success to her material prosperity. She thought of his boyish appeal to her; of what must have been his utter discomfiture in the discovery of Frida's relations to Mr. Bilson that afternoon, but more particularly of the singular change it had effected in him. How nobly and gently he had taken his loss! How much more like a man he looked in his defeat than in his passion! The element of respect which had been wanting in her previous interest in him was now present in her thoughts. It prevented her seeking him with perfunctory sympathy and worldly counsel; it made her feel strangely and unaccountably shy of any other expression.

As Mr. Bilson evidently desired to avoid local gossip until after his marriage, he had enjoined secrecy upon her, and she was also debarred from any news of Chris through his brother, who, had he known of Frida's engagement, would have naturally come to her for explanation. It also convinced her that Chris himself had not revealed anything to his brother.

III

When the news of the marriage reached Buckeye Hill, it did not, however, make much scandal, owing, possibly, to the scant number of the sex who are apt to disseminate it, and to many the name of Miss Jansen was unknown. The intelligence that Mr. Bilson would be absent for a year, and that the superior control of the Summit Hotel would devolve upon Miss Trotter, *did*, however, create a stir in that practical business community. No one doubted the wisdom of the selection. Every one knew that to Miss Trotter's tact and intellect the success of the hotel had been mainly due. Possibly, the satisfaction of Buckeye Hill was due to something else. Slowly and insensibly Miss Trotter had achieved a social distinction; the wives and daughters of the banker, the lawyer, and the pastor had made much of her, and now, as an independent woman of means, she stood first in the district. Guests deemed it an honor to have a personal interview with her. The governor of the State and the Supreme Court judges treated her like a private hostess; middle-aged Miss Trotter was considered as eligible a match as the proudest heiress in California. The old romantic fiction of her past was revived again,—they had known she was a "real lady" from the first! She received these attentions, as became her sane intellect and cool temperament, without pride, affectation, or hesitation. Only her dark eyes brightened on the day when Mr. Bilson's marriage was made known, and she was called upon by James Calton.

"I did you a great injustice," he said, with a smile.

"I don't understand you," she replied a little coldly.

"Why, this woman and her marriage," he said; "you must have known something of it all the time, and perhaps helped it along to save Chris."

"You are mistaken," returned Miss Trotter truthfully. "I knew nothing of Mr. Bilson's intentions."

"Then I have wronged you still more," he said briskly, "for I thought at first that you were inclined to help Chris in his foolishness. Now I see it was your persuasions that changed him."

"Let me tell you once for all, Mr. Calton," she returned with an impulsive heat which she regretted, "that I did not interfere in any way with your brother's suit. He spoke to me of it, and I promised to see Frida, but he afterwards asked me not to. I know nothing of the matter."

"Well," laughed Mr. Calton, "*whatever* you did, it was most efficacious, and you did it so graciously and tactfully that it has not altered his high opinion of you, if, indeed, he hasn't really transferred his affections to you."

Luckily Miss Trotter had her face turned from him at the beginning of the sentence, or he would have noticed the quick flush that suddenly came to her cheek and eyes. Yet for an instant this calm, collected woman trembled, not at what Mr. Calton might have noticed, but at what *she* had noticed in *herself.* Mr. Calton, construing her silence and averted head into some resentment of his familiar speech, continued hurriedly:—

"I mean, don't you see, that I believe no other woman could have influenced my brother as you have."

"You mean, I think, that he has taken his broken heart very lightly," said Miss Trotter, with a bitter little laugh, so unlike herself that Mr. Calton was quite concerned at it.

"No," he said gravely. "I can't say *that*! He's regularly cut up, you know! And changed; you'd hardly know him. More like a gloomy crank than the easy fool he used to be," he went on, with brotherly directness. "It wouldn't be a bad thing, you know, if you could manage to see him, Miss Trotter! In fact, as he's off his feed, and has some trouble with his arm again, owing to all this, I reckon, I've been thinking of advising him to come up to the hotel once more till he's better. So long as *she's* gone it would be all right, you know!"

By this time Miss Trotter was herself again. She reasoned, or thought she did, that this was a question of the business of the hotel, and it was clearly her duty to assent to Chris's coming. The strange yet pleasurable timidity which possessed her at the thought she ignored completely.

He came the next day. Luckily, she was so much shocked by the change in his appearance that it left no room for any other embarrassment in the meeting. His face had lost its fresh color and round outline; the lines of his mouth were drawn with pain and accented by his drooping mustache; his eyes, which had sought hers with a singular seriousness, no longer wore the look of sympathetic appeal which had once so exasperated her, but were filled with an older experience. Indeed, he seemed to have approximated so near to her own age that, by one of those paradoxes of the emotions, she felt herself much younger, and in smile and eye showed it; at which he colored faintly. But she kept her sympathy and inquiries limited to his physical health, and made no allusion to his past experiences; indeed, ignoring any connection between the two. He had been shockingly careless in his convalescence, had had a relapse in consequence, and deserved a good scolding! His relapse was a reflection upon the efficacy of the hotel as a perfect cure! She should treat him more severely now, and allow him no indulgences! I do not know that Miss Trotter intended anything covert, but their eyes met and he colored again. Ignoring this also, and promising to look after him occasionally, she quietly withdrew.

But about this time it was noticed that a change took place in Miss Trotter. Always scrupulously correct, and even severe in her dress, she allowed herself certain privileges of color, style, and material. She, who had always affected dark shades and stiff white cuffs and collars, came out in delicate tints and laces, which lent a brilliancy to her dark eyes and short crisp black curls, slightly tinged with gray. One warm summer evening she startled every one by appearing in white, possibly a reminiscence of her youth at the Vermont academy. The masculine guests thought it pretty and attractive; even the women forgave her what they believed a natural expression of her prosperity and new condition, but regretted a taste so inconsistent with her age. For all that, Miss Trotter had never looked so charming, and the faint autumnal glow in her face made no one regret her passing summer.

One evening she found Chris so much better that he was sitting on the balcony, but still so depressed that she was compelled so far to overcome the singular timidity she had felt in his presence as to ask him to come into her own little drawing-room, ostensibly to avoid the cool night air. It was the former "card-room" of the hotel, but now fitted with feminine taste and prettiness. She arranged a seat for him on the sofa, which he took with a certain brusque boyish surliness, the last vestige of his youth.

"It's very kind of you to invite me in here," he began bitterly, "when you are so run after by every one, and to leave Judge Fletcher just now to talk to me, but I suppose you are simply pitying me for being a fool!"

"I thought you were imprudent in exposing your-self to the night air on the balcony, and I think Judge Fletcher is old enough to take care of himself," she returned, with the faintest touch of coquetry, and a smile which was quite as much an amused recognition of that quality in herself as anything else.

"And I'm a baby who can't," he said angrily. After a pause he burst out abruptly: "Miss Trotter, will you answer me one question?"

"Go on," she said smilingly.

"Did you know—that—woman was engaged to Bilson when I spoke to you in the wood?"

"No!" she answered quickly, but without the sharp resentment she had shown at his brother's suggestion. "I only knew it when Mr. Bilson told me the same evening."

"And I only knew it when news came of their mar-riage," he said bitterly.

"But you must have suspected something when you saw them together in the wood," she responded.

"When I saw them together in the wood?" he re-peated dazedly.

Miss Trotter was startled, and stopped short. Was it possible he had not seen them together? She was shocked that she had spoken; but it was too late to withdraw her words. "Yes," she went on hurriedly, "I thought that was why you came back to say that I was not to speak to her."

He looked at her fixedly, and said slowly: "You thought that? Well, listen to me. I saw *no one*! I knew nothing of this! I suspected nothing! I returned before I had reached the wood—because—because—I had changed my mind!"

"Changed your mind!" she repeated wonderingly.

"Yes! Changed my mind! I couldn't stand it any longer! I did not love the girl—I never loved her—I was sick of my folly. Sick of deceiving you and myself any longer. Now you know why I didn't go into the wood, and why I didn't care where she was nor who was with her!"

"I don't understand," she said, lifting her clear eyes to his coldly.

"Of course you don't," he said bitterly. "I didn't understand myself! And when you do understand you will hate and despise me—if you do not laugh at me for a conceited fool! Hear me out, Miss Trotter, for I am speaking the truth to you now, if I never spoke it before. I never asked the girl to marry me! I never said to *her* half what I told to *you*, and when I asked you to intercede with her, I never wanted you to do it—and never expected you would."

"May I ask *why* you did it then?" said Miss Trotter,

with an acerbity which she put on to hide a vague, tantalizing consciousness.

"You would not believe me if I told you, and you would hate me if you did." He stopped, and, locking his fingers together, threw his hands over the back of the sofa and leaned toward her. "You never liked me, Miss Trotter," he said more quietly; "not from the first! From the day that I was brought to the hotel, when you came to see me, I could see that you looked upon me as a foolish, petted boy. When I tried to catch your eye, you looked at the doctor, and took your speech from him. And yet I thought I had never seen a woman so great and perfect as you were, and whose sympathy I longed so much to have. You may not believe me, but I thought you were a queen, for you were the first lady I had ever seen, and you were so different from the other girls I knew, or the women who had been kind to me. You may laugh, but it's the truth I'm telling you, Miss Trotter!"

He had relapsed completely into his old pleading, boyish way—it had struck her even as he had pleaded to her for Frida!

"I knew you didn't like me that day you came to change the bandages. Although every touch of your hands seemed to ease my pain, you did it so coldly and precisely; and although I longed to keep you there with me, you scarcely waited to take my thanks, but left me as if you had only done your duty to a stranger. And worst of all," he went on more bitterly, "the doctor knew it too—guessed how I felt toward you, and laughed at me for my hopelessness! That made me desperate, and put me up to act the fool. I did! Yes, Miss Trotter; I thought it mighty clever to appear to be in love with Frida, and to get him to ask to have her attend me regularly. And when you simply consented, without a word or thought about it and me, I knew I was nothing to you."

Miss Trotter felt a sudden thrill. The recollection of Dr. Duchesne's strange scrutiny of her, of her own mistake, which she now knew might have been the truth—flashed across her confused consciousness in swift corroboration of his words. It was a *double* revelation to her; for what else was the meaning of this subtle, insidious, benumbing sweetness that was now creeping over her sense and spirit and holding her fast. She felt she ought to listen no longer—to speak—to say something—to get up—to turn and confront him coldly—but she was powerless. Her reason told her that she had been the victim of a trick—that having deceived her once, he might be doing so again; but she could not break the spell that was upon her, nor did she want to. She must know the culmination of this confession, whose preamble thrilled her so strangely.

"The girl was kind and sympathetic," he went on, "but I was not so great a fool as not to know that she was a flirt and accustomed to attention. I suppose it was in my desperation that I told my brother, thinking he would tell you, as he did. He would not tell me what you said to him, except that you seemed to be indignant at the thought that I was only flirting with

Frida. Then I resolved to speak with you myself—and I did. I know it was a stupid, clumsy contrivance. It never seemed so stupid before I spoke to you. It never seemed so wicked as when you promised to help me, and your eyes shone on me for the first time with kindness. And it never seemed so hopeless as when I found you touched with my love for another. You wonder why I kept up this deceit until you promised. Well, I had prepared the bitter cup myself—I thought I ought to drink it to the dregs."

She turned quietly, passionately, and, standing up, faced him with a little cry. "Why are you telling me this *now*?"

He rose too, and catching her hands in his, said, with a white face, "Because I love you."

Half an hour later, when the under-housekeeper was summoned to receive Miss Trotter's orders, she found that lady quietly writing at the table. Among the orders she received was the notification that Mr. Calton's rooms would be vacated the next day. When the servant, who, like most of her class, was devoted to the good-natured, good-looking, liberal Chris, asked with some concern if the young gentleman was no better, Miss Trotter, with equal placidity, answered that it was his intention to put himself under the care of a specialist in San Francisco, and that she, Miss Trotter, fully approved of his course. She finished her letter,—the servant noticed that it was addressed to Mr.

Bilson at Paris,—and, handing it to her, bade that it should be given to a groom, with orders to ride over to the Summit post-office at once to catch the last post. As the housekeeper turned to go, she again referred to the departing guest. "It seems such a pity, ma'am, that Mr. Calton couldn't stay, as he always said you did him so much good." Miss Trotter smiled affably. But when the door closed she gave a hysterical little laugh, and then, dropping her handsome gray-streaked head in her slim hands, cried like a girl—or, indeed, as she had never cried when a girl.

When the news of Mr. Calton's departure became known the next day, some lady guests regretted the loss of this most eligible young bachelor. Miss Trotter agreed with them, with the consoling suggestion that he might return for a day or two. He did return for a day; it was thought that the change to San Francisco had greatly benefited him, though some believed he would be an invalid all his life.

Meantime Miss Trotter attended regularly to her duties, with the difference, perhaps, that she became daily more socially popular and perhaps less severe in her reception of the attentions of the masculine guests. It was finally whispered that the great Judge Boompointer was a serious rival of Judge Fletcher for her hand. When, three months later, some excitement was caused by the intelligence that Mr. Bilson was returning to take charge of his hotel, owing to the resignation of Miss Trotter, who needed a complete change, everybody knew what that meant. A few were ready to name the day when she would become Mrs. Boompointer; others had seen the engagement ring of Judge Fletcher on her slim finger.

Nevertheless Miss Trotter married neither, and by the time Mr. and Mrs. Bilson had returned she had taken her holiday, and the Summit House knew her no more.

Three years later, and at a foreign Spa, thousands of miles distant from the scene of her former triumphs, Miss Trotter reappeared as a handsome, stately, gray-haired stranger, whose aristocratic bearing deeply impressed a few of her own countrymen who witnessed her arrival, and believed her to be a grand duchess at the least. They were still more convinced of her superiority when they saw her welcomed by the well-known Baroness X., and afterwards engaged in a very confidential conversation with that lady. But they would have been still more surprised had they known the tenor of that conversation.

"I am afraid you will find the Spa very empty just now," said the baroness critically. "But there are a few of your compatriots here, however, and they are always amusing. You see that somewhat faded blonde sitting quite alone in that arbor? That is her position day after day, while her husband openly flirts or is flirted with by half the women here. Quite the opposite experience one has of American women, where it's all the other way, is it not? And there is an odd story about her which may account for, if it does not excuse, her husband's neglect. They're very rich, but they say she was originally a mere servant in a hotel."

"You forget that I told you I was once only a house-keeper in one," said Miss Trotter, smiling.

"Nonsense. I mean that this woman was a mere peasant, and frightfully ignorant at that!"

Miss Trotter put up her eyeglass, and, after a moment's scrutiny, said gently, "I think you are a little severe. I know her; it's a Mrs. Bilson."

"No, my dear. You are quite wrong. That was the name of her *first* husband. I am told she was a widow who married again—quite a fascinating young man, and evidently her superior—that is what is so funny. She is a Mrs. Calton—'Mrs. Chris Calton,' as she calls herself."

"Is her husband—Mr. Calton—here?" said Miss Trotter after a pause, in a still gentler voice.

"Naturally not. He has gone on an excursion with a party of ladies to the Schwartzberg. He returns to-morrow. You will find *her* very stupid, but *he* is very jolly, though a little spoiled by women. Why do we always spoil them?"

Miss Trotter smiled, and presently turned the subject. But the baroness was greatly disappointed to find the next day that an unexpected telegram had obliged Miss Trotter to leave the Spa without meeting the Caltons.

www.ingramcontent.com/pod-product-compliance
Lightning Source LLC
Chambersburg PA
CBHW060735180626
46819CB00001B/34